Savannah Spectator Blind Item

Readers, we all know that a secretive and seductively handsome desert prince has lived within our midsts for several years now. And try as they might, not one of our Southern belles has been able to break down the walls of solitude surrounding him. But like out of an Arabian fairy tale, our sheikh has fallen for forbidden fruit…not exactly a commoner, but not royalty surely—except maybe to us Savannahians.

The lady in question has a famous last name and has been staying at the royal stables under the guise of horseback riding lessons! But from the way they've been spotted carrying on, a horse is not the only animal the sheikh's been teaching her to ride. Did I really just *say* that? Oh, well, must be the June heat….

Dear Reader,

Welcome to another passion-filled month at Silhouette Desire—where we guarantee powerful and provocative love stories you are sure to enjoy. We continue our fabulous DYNASTIES: THE DANFORTHS series with Kristi Gold's *Challenged by the Sheikh*—her intensely ardent hero will put your senses on overload. More hot heroes are on the horizon when *USA TODAY* bestselling author Ann Major returns to Silhouette Desire with the dramatic story of *The Bride Tamer*.

Ever wonder what it would be like to be a man's mistress— even just for pretend? Well, the heroine of Katherine Garbera's *Mistress Minded* finds herself just in that predicament when she agrees to help out her sexy-as-sin boss in the next KING OF HEARTS title. Jennifer Greene brings us the second story in THE SCENT OF LAVENDER, her compelling series about the Campbell sisters, with *Wild In the Moonlight*—and this is one hero to go wild for! If it's a heartbreaker you're looking for, look no farther than *Hold Me Tight* by Cait London as she continues her HEARTBREAKERS miniseries with this tale of one sexy male specimen on the loose. And looking for a little *Hot Contact* himself is the hero of Susan Crosby's latest book in her BEHIND CLOSED DOORS series; this sinfully seductive police investigator always gets his woman! Thank goodness.

And thank *you* for coming back to Silhouette Desire every month. Be sure to join us next month for *New York Times* bestselling author Lisa Jackson's *Best-Kept Lies,* the highly anticipated conclusion to her wildly popular series THE McCAFFERTYS.

Keep on reading!

Melissa Jeglinski

Melissa Jeglinski
Senior Editor, Silhouette Desire

Please address questions and book requests to:
Silhouette Reader Service
U.S.: 3010 Walden Ave., P.O. Box 1325, Buffalo, NY 14269
Canadian: P.O. Box 609, Fort Erie, Ont. L2A 5X3

DYNASTIES : THE DANFORTHS

CHALLENGED BY THE SHEIKH
KRISTI GOLD

Silhouette®

Desire

Published by Silhouette Books
America's Publisher of Contemporary Romance

Special thanks and acknowledgment are given to Kristi Gold for her contribution to the DYNASTIES: THE DANFORTHS series.

To the wonderful "Danforth Divas"; it's been a pleasure working with you all. And a special thank-you to Shirley Rogers for her invaluable input during the development of our stories.

 SILHOUETTE BOOKS

ISBN 0-373-76585-1

CHALLENGED BY THE SHEIKH

Copyright © 2004 by Harlequin Books S.A.

This edition published by arrangement with Harlequin Books S.A.

® and TM are trademarks of Harlequin Books S.A., used under license. Trademarks indicated with ® are registered in the United States Patent and Trademark Office, the Canadian Trade Marks Office and in other countries.

Visit Silhouette Books at www.eHarlequin.com

Printed in U.S.A.

Books by Kristi Gold

Silhouette Desire

Cowboy for Keeps #1308
Doctor for Keeps #1320
His Sheltering Arms #1350
Her Ardent Sheikh #1358
*Dr. Dangerous #1415
*Dr. Desirable #1421
*Dr. Destiny #1427
His E-Mail Order Wife #1454
The Sheikh's Bidding #1485
*Renegade Millionaire #1497
Marooned with a Millionaire #1517
Expecting the Sheikh's Baby #1531
Fit for a Sheikh #1576
Challenged by the Sheikh #1585

*Marrying an M.D.

KRISTI GOLD

has always believed that love has remarkable healing powers and feels very fortunate to be able to weave stories of romance and commitment. As a bestselling author and a Romance Writers of America RITA® Award finalist, she's learned that although accolades are wonderful, the most cherished rewards come from the most unexpected places, namely from personal stories shared by readers.

You can reach Kristi at KGOLDAUTHOR@aol.com, through her Web site at http://kristigold.com or snail mail at P.O. Box 9070, Waco, TX 76714. (Please include an SASE for a response.)

DYNASTIES: THE DANFORTHS

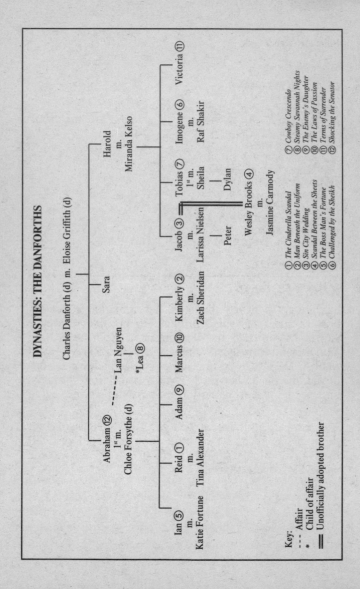

Charles Danforth (d) m. Eloise Griffith (d)

Sara

Abraham ⑫
1ˢᵗ m.
Chloe Forsythe (d)

--- Lan Nguyen
|
*Lea ⑧

Reid ①
m.
Tina Alexander

Ian ⑤
m.
Katie Fortune

Adam ⑨

Marcus ⑩

Kimberly ②
m.
Zach Sheridan

Harold
m.
Miranda Kelso

Jacob ③
m.
Larissa Nielsen

Peter

Wesley Brooks ④
m.
Jasmine Carmody

Tobias ⑦
1ˢᵗ m.
Sheila

Dylan

Imogene ⑥
m.
Raf Shakir

Victoria ⑪

① *The Cinderella Scandal*
② *Man Beneath the Uniform*
③ *Sin City Wedding*
④ *Scandal Between the Sheets*
⑤ *The Boss Man's Fortune*
⑥ *Challenged by the Sheikh*
⑦ *Cowboy Crescendo*
⑧ *Steamy Savannah Nights*
⑨ *The Enemy's Daughter*
⑩ *The Laws of Passion*
⑪ *Terms of Surrender*
⑫ *Shocking the Senator*

Key:
- - - Affair
* Child of affair
═══ Unofficially adopted brother

One

The search for premiere horseflesh had brought Imogene Danforth to SaHráa Stables. The discovery of prime man flesh had been a very definite plus.

She stood outside the open stall door watching the stranger's bare back as he shoveled shavings onto the floor, spreading them meticulously over the rubber matting. A rivulet of sweat slid down between his shoulder blades and tracked the pearl path of his spine before disappearing below the waistband of a pair of well-worn jeans. Those jeans and the tear right below the back pocket, his tensile muscle covered by warm sand-toned skin, garnered Imogene's complete attention.

Unfortunately, thoroughly examining a stable hand's assets was not on her agenda, even if he did have a landmark butt and expansive shoulders. Leasing a four-legged foe was her goal, even though her knowledge of the equine species could be compiled on the head of an amoeba. In fact, the last time she'd ridden a horse, she'd been five years old and the pony had managed to buck her off. And the last time she'd been involved with a man, he'd thrown her over for a more suitable partner. So when it came to horses and men, Imogene hadn't been too lucky in either instance. But she could still appreciate both, regardless of her less-than-happy history. However, her appearance here today was strictly business.

The dust kicking up from the shavings tickled Imogene's sensitive nose. No doubt, she was going to start sneezing in rapid succession. She never did anything halfway; this was no exception.

After five or so obnoxious *ah-choos,* Imogene muttered ''Excuse me,'' in apology and greeting as she took a tissue from her pocket and dabbed at her watering eyes, hoping her mascara had remained intact, otherwise she would be more raccoon than woman. Once her vision cleared, she directed her attention on the stable hand to find he had turned to give her a full-frontal view.

He was phenomenally tall and predictably gorgeous with tousled raven hair, a straight-edge nose and a shading of whiskers framing full lips that Imogene would wager had seen lots of action in the kissing department. His chiseled chest revealed the results of physical labor as well as a spattering of dark hair. The jeans began right below his navel, offering a glimpse of what Imogene's brothers used to call The Happy Trail, a path of hair leading to that part of the male anatomy that made men very happy to be men. And admittedly, made many women glad to be women— as long as a man did not utilize it as his primary brain.

Imogene finally traveled back to his eyes—thunderstorm-gray eyes rimmed with an almost black perimeter. Seductive eyes that surveyed her with barefaced interest, the same way she had blatantly assessed him.

"How may I help you?" he asked in a moderately deep voice that was darkly lyrical and surprisingly sophisticated.

Imogene could think of several responses, none that would be fitting for a woman who needed to keep her mind on her business, not on his butt. "I'm looking for Sheikh Shakir."

He braced both palms on the shovel's handle, highlighting the prominent veins on his arms. "Is he expecting you?"

Imogene obviously should have called first, but there hadn't been time. She'd found the stable on the Internet, discovered it was the closest to Savannah and then rushed out of the office. Besides, if she had called, only to find the owner wasn't available, then she would have missed out on this manly panorama standing before her. "Actually, I didn't make an appointment. I hope that won't be a problem since the sign out front says Visitors Welcome."

"That would depend on what you want from him."

"I need a good Arabian, and fast," she blurted before she realized how questionable that sounded. Where was her brain? Back in the Beemer?

His smile arrived gradually. A somewhat sardonic smile but patently sensual as his gaze raked over her, from blond bangs to sensible pumps, lingering at her legs and breasts. "I am Arabian, and I can be very good."

Saints above, he was flirting with her, literally baring her body and soul with a few choice looks and suggestive words. Oddly enough, Imogene wanted to flirt back. But she couldn't, or shouldn't. "I appreciate the offer, but I was referring to an Arabian *horse*."

He shifted his weight from one leg to the other while Imogene did the same, her heels digging into the artificial green turf covering the aisle—appropriate, considering the barn was as big as a football field.

"Are you interested in breeding?" he asked.

What a novel idea. Unfortunately, that was not on the agenda, either. "Excuse me?"

"Are you looking for breeding stock? Perhaps a stallion?"

"Actually, I'm looking for someone to ride." Someone? Oh, jeez. "I mean, I need a horse to ride."

His grin deepened, reflecting a trace of amusement and a very definite, very sexy charm. "How much experience do you have?"

Although she assumed he'd meant equestrian experience, his provocative tone indicated he might mean something else altogether, and so did the heat in his eyes. "I have some experience." Just a slight stretch of the truth, especially where horses and men were concerned.

He leaned the shovel against the wall then folded his arms across his chest. "Would you want a gentle mount? Or are you comfortable with something more daring?"

Imogene was suddenly assailed by the image of taking a wild ride with this particular stud. A long, wild ride. She inclined her head and gave him a coy look, greatly enjoying the exchange. After all, what harm could it do? She would probably never see him again after today. It sure beat the heck out of her usual money-matters conversations with men. "Whatever I need to stay in the saddle for more than a few minutes."

"That can be achieved with practice."

"Then I'm assuming you've had a lot of practice?"

"Undeniably."

What a confident cad. An incredibly stunning, confident cad.

Oh, Lordy, she had the hots for a stable hand. Her parents would certainly love that. But as much as Imogene wanted to continue playing this innuendo game, she didn't have time. She needed to find a horse and report back to her slug of a boss, Sid Carver, who'd gotten her into this mess by telling prospective clients she was an equestrienne extraordinaire. Next month, she was to join her client and his wife at their farm with her own show-quality Arabian, pretending to be a hotshot rider as well as a hotshot investment banker. Had it not been for the possibility of a promotion, she would never have stepped foot in a stable and risked stepping in something not at all pleasant.

But she would have to agree that the man before her was a positive. Still, she needed to meet with his boss and get the show on the road so she could get back on the road. She needed to quit fantasizing about his big hands and feet, his deadly smile and the fact that he'd hooked his thumbs in his pockets, drawing her attention to a place she had no good reason to go. But, oh, did she want to go there.

Straightening her jacket lapels and her shoulders, Imogene forced herself back into professional mode and her gaze back to his face. "I need to meet with the sheikh to discuss leasing one of his better horses."

His expression turned suddenly serious. "I assure you that Sheikh Shakir does not lease his quality stock to someone off the street. He would have to know more about your intentions."

So much for fun and games. "I understand, so now if you'll go get him, we can begin to negotiate."

He retrieved his discarded denim shirt from the handle of the wheelbarrow then slipped it on without bothering to button it. "If you will follow me, I'll show you to his private office where you may wait for his return."

"Good enough. Just lead the way."

He passed by her on a wave of heat, and the scent of sawdust and sweat combined with a trace of sandalwood cologne—pheromone-laden smells that had Imogene's recently inactive libido in an uproar.

She followed behind him to ascend a staircase, gauging every roll of his narrow hips that caused the torn fabric below his pocket to part even more, but not quite enough to get a substantial view of the upward curve of his buttock from the top of his thigh. Now if he could just manage to tear it open a tiny bit more…

Apparently her hormones had hijacked her common sense. Strictly business, she silently chanted with every step she took.

Once they reached the top, he opened the door to a small apartment complete with brown suede furniture, a small kitchenette, an office partially concealed by French doors and a hallway that most likely led to a bedroom or two. She wondered if that would be a stopover on the grand tour.

Obviously not since he showed her to the living area and gestured to a chair that faced the door. "Make yourself comfortable while you wait. You are welcome to any refreshments in the refrigerator."

"Thanks." She looked around the room because it was simply too tempting to look at him. "This is a very nice place. Does the sheikh come in here often?"

"Yes."

She brought her attention back to him. "Do you live on the premises?"

"Yes."

His brief answers indicated he was no longer willing to carry on a conversation, or carry on at all. Just as well since Imogene had more pressing—albeit mundane—issues to attend to. "Well, thanks, Mr.…." She frowned. "I'm sorry, I didn't catch your name."

"Nor I yours, but perhaps it would be best if we kept it that way."

He turned and walked out the door, leaving Imogene alone with the assumption that he'd probably been told that the sheikh's female clients were hands off. She would definitely like to get her hands on him and take a few things off.

She sank back in the chair and sighed. What in the world was wrong with her? Sure, she'd been in a dating drought of late, ever since her breakup with Wayne well over a year ago.

Dear CPA Wayne, who liked his women with finer feminine qualities, and who had found Imogene lacking in that respect. A Magnolia blossom Imogene was not, nor would she ever be. She'd always preferred business suits to ball gowns. Preferred premium stocks to proms. And she had no intention of getting involved again with someone who had unrealistic expectations of how she should think and act. She loved her job and she intended to stick to it, climbing her way up the proverbial corporate ladder whatever it might take, even if she didn't have much of a social life.

But, hey, she wore skirts now and then, like today, a really ridiculous thing to do considering she had to traipse around in a barn. But since she hadn't been given much notice, she hadn't had time to change. From now on, she would wear slacks, especially in a barn. Not that she intended to visit any on a regular basis.

However, the man dearth still didn't excuse her horny reaction to the stable boy. Stable *man,* she corrected. All man. Every bit of him, and she suspected that he was six feet tall plus a good four inches. Much more, if she counted his…

Good heavens. She tipped her head back in the chair and rolled her eyes to the ceiling. How ridiculous. Her life was much too hectic to include silly fantasies about some stranger's manhood.

Imogene closed her eyes, intending to regroup since sleep had been at a premium lately and she needed to have sharp wits about her. Instead, she only saw Mr. Stable Man. After at least ten minutes of attempting to go over a mental laundry list of what needed to be said when she met with the sheikh, she finally gave up and let her daydream take flight. No one would have to know where her thoughts were leading. No one would suspect that her imagination had taken her back into that stall where all conversation was suspended, giving way to forbidden foreplay with a very tall, very well equipped manly man.

Although her logical side tried to convince her that this was not the time or the place to immerse herself in a sexual scenario, Imogene continued to play out the scene in her mind.

After all, what better way to spend the time while she waited? No one would ever have to know, least of all the stable hand.

Sheikh Rafi ibn Shakir knew women very well. He knew what made them sigh, what made them tremble, what made them weep. He knew how to heighten their gratification as he sought each erogenous zone with both his hands and his mouth. He knew the look of bliss in a lover's face, and he had known the pleasure of watching a lover sleep. Therefore he recognized that the woman he now observed from the apartment doorway had her eyes closed, but she was definitely not sleeping. Nor was she aware of his appearance. He intended to keep it that way, at least for a few more moments.

On the surface she appeared to be all-business despite her chin-length golden-blond hair and attractive features. Yet as he watched her slide her tongue over her bottom lip and her hand graze her stocking-covered thigh below the hem of her black skirt, he was convinced that a sensual being resided beneath the professional image.

Without opening her eyes, she released the button on her tailored jacket, allowing it to fall open to reveal a white silk blouse. A soft sigh escaped her lips as she laid one palm over her bare flesh where the blouse parted at the collar. Her respiration increased, evident by the rise and fall of her breasts as her fingertips brushed across her chest, moving farther and farther beneath the fabric. And with each pass of her hand, Raf imagined his own hand there. His hands everywhere on her body. That thought made him shift against the tightness building in his groin and the temptation to join her.

Some might think him arrogant to assume that she was in the throes of a fantasy involving them, together. Yet he had good intuition when it came to the opposite sex and solid instincts when it came to chemistry between a man and a woman. That chemistry had been very apparent in the stall when she had assessed him with inquisitive emerald eyes. That chemistry was still apparent as he continued to watch her, knowing she was very vulnerable at the moment and quite possibly open to making the fantasy reality. If he were less controlled, he would drop to his knees before her, slide his hands beneath her skirt and discover exactly how her body was reacting to her current musings. He would open his pants, relieving him of his discomfort, part her legs and take her right there where she sat.

As enticing as that prospect might be, honor bound him to make his presence known even though he would prefer to continue to see how far she would go before she recognized she was no longer alone. To see how long his own neglected need would allow him to only observe her before he tossed caution to the wind. Not too long, he decided as her legs slightly parted and her fingertips drew a path up and down the inside of her knee.

When he reached behind him and tripped the lock on the door, her eyes snapped open, she gripped the chair's arms and her frame went rigid.

Her gaze met his, mortification in her startled expression. "I didn't hear you come in," she said in a raspy voice.

He took a step forward and affected casualness even though he was not unaffected by what he had witnessed. "I was reluctant to disturb you since you seemed to be enjoying your *nap*."

She glanced away but not before he saw a flash of guilt in her eyes. "I guess I drifted off." She shifted in the seat. "This is a very comfortable chair."

And Raf was more than uncomfortable. In an effort to hide his own reaction, he took a seat on the small sofa facing her and crossed one leg over the other.

"I almost didn't recognize you in the khakis and polo," she said while she surveyed the room as if afraid to look at him.

"Are you saying you do not like my attire now?" Why that mattered to Raf at all, he did not have a clue. But for some strange reason, her opinion did matter.

She finally brought her attention back to him. "Actually, you look more natural in jeans, not that I'm complaining."

If she only knew he had exchanged his royal trappings for casual attire not more than two years ago when he'd come to America. He had no intention of enlightening her yet. "Exactly why are you here?"

She tugged at her skirt. "I've already told you why I'm here. I need a horse. Now I need to talk to the owner."

Raf needed to keep his eyes off her breasts, and to reveal the truth. "I am the owner."

"You're not serious." Her eyes widened with awareness. "You're Sheikh Shakir?"

"Sheikh Rafi ibn Shakir."

Her astonishment gave way to irritation. "Oh, really? So how am I to address you? Sheikh? Your Highness? I certainly don't want to step on your royal toes."

Her sarcasm both amused and intrigued him. "You may call me Raf."

"Is that Rafe with an *e* on the end?"

"No *e* on the end. Why do you ask?"

She crossed her arms beneath her breasts and lifted her chin. "I'm just trying to get everything straight."

Raf ignored the venom in her tone. "And you are?"

"Confused as to why you were passing yourself off as a worker," she said. "Unless, of course, you're lying to me now. So which is it? Sheikh or stable boy?"

The accusation did not sit well with Raf, although he supposed he could understand her suspicion. "I assure you, I am the owner of SaHráa Stables. And I am not a boy."

"That's obvious," she said, a tinge of color rising to her cheeks.

"You have still not told me your name."

"Ms. Danforth."

Raf leaned back in the chair and streaked a hand over his jaw. "Would that be any relation to senatorial candidate Abraham Danforth?"

"He's my uncle. My father's brother."

"Both involved in the Danforth coffee dynasty?"

"Yes, but my father's retired now."

For all intents and purposes, Ms. Danforth was most likely an heiress, although very unlike those Raf had encountered since his arrival in Georgia. He found it somewhat refreshing that she obviously was not here because of his money or his position. Perhaps she would be interested in what he could offer in terms of pleasure, but that would be unwise to ask. At the moment she did not look amenable to any suggestions of that nature. "I have contributed to your uncle's campaign on several occasions. I greatly respect him."

Her smile appeared self-conscious and somewhat forced. "We appreciate your support. Where are you originally from?"

"A small country called Amythra, near Oman."

"What brought you to Georgia, if you don't mind me asking?"

He did, yet he would offer her some courtesy. "I have no ties to my country as I am not in line to inherit the kingdom. I have found Savannah to be a prime location for horse breeding. Does that sufficiently answer your question?"

"Yes, but now I need something else from you."

Raf had no doubt she needed several things from him, considering her earlier state. "You are requiring a horse?"

"That's right. And I need it soon."

And he needed more information. "How long have you been riding, Ms. Danforth?"

Her gaze drifted away as her hands tightened together in her lap. "Actually, it's been quite a while since I've ridden."

He did not like the sound of that. "Exactly how long?"

She hesitated a few moments. "About twenty years."

"And your age now?"

"Twenty-five, almost twenty-six."

The woman was apparently devoid of common sense. "Then you were no more than a child when you last rode?"

She met his gaze head-on. "Yes, but it's not too late for me to learn."

"I refuse to sell or lease any of my stock to a novice rider." For reasons he dared not reveal to her. Reasons that served to unearth emotional pain he'd worked hard to bury.

She moved to the edge of her seat and sent him a pleading look. "Sheikh Shakir, I'm desperate. I'm an investment banker and I have three weeks to obtain a horse and learn to ride in order to impress a prospective client who believes I'm an expert rider."

"I admire your commitment to your work, but was it necessary to go to such extremes as to lie to these clients?"

Her eyes narrowed, full of feminine fire. "And was it

necessary for you to lie about your identity when we met in the barn?''

Unfortunately, she had him on that. ''I suppose we both have our reasons for concealing the truth. That will not change my mind about leasing you a horse, since you do not have the proper training.''

''If I take some lessons, then you'll reconsider?''

''Perhaps, if you can prove to me you have the appropriate skills.''

She paused a moment before saying, ''Is there a possibility that you could teach me?''

He most definitely could teach her many things. ''Three weeks would not be enough time for you to master proper riding.''

Frustration returned to her face. ''Don't you have an old nag who's been around the block a time or two?''.

''I do not possess any nags. I have only superior stock.''

''Then you're saying that you don't have one broken-in, gentle, older horse that I could learn on?''

He did have one in particular, a gelding that was up in years and too tired to have much spirit. ''It is possible.''

She looked somewhat hopeful and much too sensual for Raf to ignore. ''Then you'll consider giving me lessons?''

''Would that involve only the horse?''

She hinted at a smile, yet it did not quite develop. ''What makes you think I would need lessons in anything else?''

''Forgive me if I am wrong in my assumptions.''

''You are forgiven for that and the fact you initially lied to me. If you'll consider my request.''

A born negotiator, Raf decided. But so was he. ''You said you are an investment banker?''

''Yes. Right now I'm with a regional I-bank. But I plan to work my way up and eventually go to New York to play with the big boys.''

He wondered how willing she would be to play at passion. For the past two years he'd purposefully avoided women with questionable intentions, yet he did not wish to avoid this one. "We could possibly work out an exchange in services, since you, too, have something that I want."

She crossed one shapely leg over the other and smoothed a hand over her skirt. "Exactly what do you have in mind?"

He had many things on his mind, most having nothing to do with business. He wondered how her skin would feel against his palms. How she would taste. How her body would feel surrounding his. "I would like your professional opinion on some possible investment strategies."

"I could do that. So does this mean we've reached an agreement?"

Raf thought a moment, and although he recognized he could be entering into a dangerous pact, he was willing to risk it since he understood all too well that good business led to desperate measures. Granted, he had to admit that he found Ms. Danforth very appealing. Yet her apparent strong will concerned him greatly, at least when it came to riding lessons. He would simply have to outline the rules. If she refused to follow them, then he would rescind his offer.

Raf came to his feet and extended his hand, which she took without hesitation. "I would be willing to teach you how to ride."

Her smile deepened, highlighting the delicate features of her face. Her hand was smooth against his calloused palm and he could imagine how it would feel against his bare flesh.

"Great," she said, and after a hearty handshake, rose to stand face-to-face with him, almost too close for Raf to concentrate.

"I do have several conditions," he added. "You must abide by my rules in terms of how you handle the horse.

Safety is of the utmost importance. If you disobey me, then I will call off the arrangement.''

"I'll be cooperative.''

He had some doubts about that. "I would also like to know your given name. I feel that we should be informal if we are to work together.''

"It's Imogene.''

He frowned. "That does not suit you.''

"I beg your pardon?''

"My intent was not to insult you. I simply do not believe the name serves you well.''

She lifted her chin in defiance. "I was named after my mother's favorite great-aunt who happened to be quite a businesswoman in her day, before she joined the convent.''

Raf could not quell his smile. "Your namesake was a nun?''

"Yes, she was. A very good one, too.''

"But you chose not to follow her path.''

"Do I look like I have?''

"Most definitely not.'' She did look as if she would like to flog him, apparent from the antagonism in her eyes. That admittedly excited Raf, although he decided he should temper his comments.

"As I was saying,'' he continued. "I appreciate the importance of one's heritage, but I still do not believe your name suits you.'' Unable to stop himself, he reached over and pushed away a tendril of blond hair from her cheek. "You have very magical eyes, therefore I will call you Genie.''

Her anger gave way to shock. "What did you say?''

"Genie. That suits you much better.'' Her expression heralded a sadness and vulnerability Raf could not understand, or ignore. "Is there a reason why you do not wish to be called that?''

She shook her head. "No. It's fine. It's just that someone special used to call me Genie."

Raf suspected that someone was a man and that he was not completely gone from her memory. For a brief moment he considered ways to drive the former suitor from her mind. "If it would make you uncomfortable for me to call you—"

"No. Really. I like that name much better than Imogene. Besides, I'm going to need some heavy-duty magic in order to learn to ride in three weeks."

He would willingly show her all the magic a man and woman could share, should the situation arise. "Then we are agreed on that point, Genie."

Thankfully, her smile returned, this time more relaxed. "Is there anything else, since I need to get back to work?"

"We have not discussed the particulars of the lessons."

"You're right. I plan to come here around 5:00 p.m. every day and stay until around six before I head back to Savannah. Longer on the weekends if I'm not traveling during the week for my job."

"That will not do. If you are to learn in such a small amount of time, you will need to train at least twice a day."

"I can't do that with my work. Not to mention, I live in Savannah. You're basically in the middle of nowhere."

The alternate plan that unfolded in Raf's mind could be considered imprudent, yet full of interesting possibilities. "Then I see no other recourse than to change your plans."

"Are you withdrawing the offer?"

"No. I am saying that for the next three weeks, you must live with me."

"But—"

"I will see you first thing in the morning. Be prepared to work."

Raf left the room before she could issue another protest. Before he did something rash such as kiss the stunned look off her face. Kiss her into silence. As much as he would like to do that, he thought it best to keep his mouth occupied by giving her instructions on the finer points of horsemanship—and ignore her finer female points.

That could prove difficult if she agreed to reside with him for the next three weeks. If his instincts continued to serve him well, he predicted she would.

Live with him? Ha!

"How ludicrous," Imogene muttered as she steered her sedan around the corner and headed down her street. She certainly had no good reason to reside with a man she barely knew. She couldn't imagine what she would have to gain by doing that. Oh, she could imagine gaining quite a bit in terms of a little activity between the sheets. But that shouldn't concern her, nor should it be the basis for her agreeing to something so preposterous as living with him. After all, this was business and nothing more.

Of course she was going to do it, move in with him tomorrow morning. What other choice did she have? If she couldn't get him to agree to the terms any other way, then she would just have to sacrifice a little of her time, even take vacation days if she had to, although she shouldn't have to. After all, Sid had insisted she do this. And Sid had better cooperate or else. Or else what? She was going to quit her job? Not an option. No man was going to force her out of her position during the height of her burgeoning career.

The minute Imogene pulled into the parking lot of the condo, she hopped out of the car, let herself in and immediately grabbed the phone to call her boss. She pounded out his private cell phone number and he answered with an irritable, "Carver here. State your business."

She dropped down on the chintz sofa, kicked off her heels and said, "Sid, it's Imogene."

"Where have you been all afternoon?" he barked.

Fortunately, Sid's bark was worse than his bite. Not that she would ever get close enough to him to let him bite her. "I've been looking into leasing a horse to impress the Granthams next month, as you requested."

"Any luck?" At least he sounded somewhat nicer.

"Actually, yes. But in order to pull this off, I have to take some riding lessons."

"Riding lessons? How hard could it be, Danforth? All you gotta do is sit on a saddle. The horse does all the work."

Sid's attitude did not surprise Imogene in the least. In their relationship, she was the pack mule, he rode her constantly and she did all the work while he basked in the glory. "Look, it's not that simple. I have to take some lessons in order to be convincing. The owner of the stable has agreed to lease me one of his Arabians and he also offered to teach me."

"Okay," Sid said. "So you take a few riding lessons after business hours. That's not a big deal, I guess."

Here goes. "I can't do it after work, Sid. Considering I only have three weeks to become a pro, and this particular place is an hour away, I'm going to be living at the stables."

"No way, Imogene. You can't take off just like that."

"I haven't had a vacation in the two years I've been there. But I should be paid since it's work related. If I do this well, then we'll have the Granthams' business and that will be a feather in your cap." Imogene would like to tell him what to do with that feather—shove it where the grass doesn't grow.

His rough sigh filtered through the line, and Imogene could picture him slouching on his couch, rubbing his belly and his bald head simultaneously, the only two things he could do at once since Sid Carver was anything but a multitasker. He was, however, the bank president's son-in-law.

"Okay," he finally said. "If this is the only way you can do this, then I'll let you have the time off. But if I can't take up your slack, then you have to cut it short and come back to work."

Not if he couldn't reach her. "Agreed."

"Where can I reach you?"

Drat. "I'll be at Saîlráa Stables about fifty miles away. I'll keep my cell phone on." Unless she accidentally forgot to charge it, on purpose.

"Is that the place owned by that sheikh?"

"Yes, it is. He'll be instructing me."

Sid's cynical laugh grated on Imogene's nerves. "I just bet he'd like to instruct you—on several things. If you have to sleep with the guy, do it. Maybe we can get his business, too."

Of all the unscrupulous jackasses. "I'm not going to sleep with him for the sake of commerce, Sid." Now, for the sake of pure pleasure, she might actually consider that.

Business, Imogene. Strictly business.

"I'll see you in three weeks, Danforth. I'm counting on you. C & G's counting on you. You don't want to disappoint us."

"I won't."

When Sid hung up, Imogene hoped she could keep the promise, since she wasn't immune to disappointing people. Five years ago she had let down the one person who had meant the world to her—her baby sister, Victoria. If she had thought about someone else's needs, not only her own, then maybe Tori would be here now instead of taking her place in a police file among all the other missing persons who had disappeared without a trace.

No, she wouldn't disappoint Sid the way she had disappointed her family. Oh, her mom and dad and brothers had never accused her of being responsible for Tori's disappearance. In fact, they hadn't blamed her at all. But Imogene had blamed herself. She still did. Immersing herself in the high excitement of big business had served as a means to escape, and most of the time it had worked.

Yet today, when Raf Shakir had called her Genie—the label Victoria had given her because she couldn't say Imogene—the pain of her past, the horrible loss, had come rushing back on a riptide of emotion. And somehow the sheikh had seen through her tough-gal guise.

Imogene would have to remember not to be so emotionally exposed in his presence again. No matter how attractive she found him, no matter how much she would like to know him better, she could never let him see those sad, sad secrets that haunted her heart as surely as the ghosts haunted Crofthaven, her uncle Abraham's stately mansion.

Imogene Danforth would never let Sheikh Raf Shakir know about the sins of her past. She would be an exemplary student and prove to him that she could meet the challenge. She refused to disappoint another person again.

Two

The next morning, Imogene drove down the lengthy road lined with long-armed live oaks, white rail fencing and pristine paddocks for the second time in two days. She bypassed the path leading to the stables and turned into the circular drive in front of the traditional white plantation house with plantation shutters and plantation grace. The elaborate farm was truly an oasis in the midst of a no-man's-land, situated not far from a small river with an unpronounceable name and surrounded by swamps. Cotton Creek, the closest town—if you could call it that—was over twenty miles away.

After exiting her BMW with bags in tow, she rang the bell adjacent to the double walnut doors and waited an interminable amount of time for someone to answer her summons. That someone came in the form of a sixty-something lady.

She was Southern through and through, from her moderately big brown hair to her peony-painted lips. She wore a crisp pink blouse, a full gray below-the-knee skirt and a string of pearls that most likely had been passed down through generations of well-mannered ladies until they'd landed around her plump throat.

Imogene smiled, said, "Hello, I'm looking for Raf Shakir," then waited for the classic Georgia drawl and the word *sugar*.

"What the hell do you want with him?"

So much for Southern charm. "He invited me here. I'm to be his guest for the next three weeks."

The woman let go a sarcastic laugh second only to Sid's in the annoyance department. "They always say that."

Imogene frowned. "They?"

"All the women who flock to this place like honeybees to hairspray, sugar."

Aha! Sugar was in her vocabulary, if not in her disposition. "I'm not one of them," Imogene quickly added. "I'm here on business."

"They all say that, too. Besides, it's Saturday. No one does business on a Saturday."

Obviously Miss Crotchety had no idea what went on in the corporate world. "I promise I'm only here to learn to ride a horse. Ask Sheikh Shakir. He'll verify that for you. In fact, he's expecting me."

She looked more than a tad suspicious. "He didn't tell me anything about you. Besides, he's not here."

Great. "Where is he?"

"Where do you think he is?"

Imogene felt as if she'd entered Fort Knox, not a horse farm. Maybe she needed a password. She thought of several snippy ones. "I have no idea where he is. Maybe in the stable?"

"Probably so, out playing in the manure. The man would

rather be working like a field hand than acting like a prince.''

"I hadn't even considered him being a prince,'' Imogene voiced aloud, much to her chagrin.

The woman looked as though Imogene had left her brain hanging among the Spanish moss draped on the ancient oaks. "His blood is bluer than blue, simple as that, and he doesn't take too kindly to women with their sights set on his checkbook.''

Imogene raised her hand in oath. "I swear to you that I don't care about his wallet." Maybe his stock portfolio, but only from a business standpoint. She had a sizable trust fund, plus her salary, so she wasn't in need of a benefactor. She did have to admit he had other assets that interested her, something she didn't dare reveal to anyone, especially Miss No Manners.

"Then you must be interested in what else he keeps in his pants,'' the woman stated, followed by a devilish grin.

Imogene bit her tongue, literally. "Look…ma'am, if you could just track your boss down for me, we'll have this cleared up in no time.''

"Oh, hell, why not,'' she said and stepped aside. "I can't keep playing Plantation police. I have too much to do trying to run this house. Come in and pull up a chair in the parlor. I'll see if I can find him.''

Imogene followed her to said parlor and took a seat on the blue sateen settee, bags at her feet and hands joined primly in her lap. "I really appreciate this, ma'am.''

"Call me Doris. Who are you?''

Imogene didn't bother to extend her hand considering Doris still didn't look at all trusting. "Imogene Danforth from Savannah.''

Doris's brown eyes went as wide as a vault. "Danforth? Are you kin to that handsome Senator Abraham Danforth?''

Good old Uncle Abe. He'd opened plenty of doors for Imogene, including those that had led to her job. "He's my uncle, but he's not a senator yet."

Doris patted her hair and it didn't move an inch. "Oh, he will be, you mark my words. He'll get all the women's votes, mine included. As far as I'm concerned, he could campaign backward and that would be fine by me because I could get a real good look at his very fine fanny."

Maybe Imogene had something in common with Doris after all, at least in terms of an appreciation for manly buttocks. "Yes, my uncle is a very attractive man. But he's an even better leader, or will be." If he survived the nasty campaign.

Imogene half expected Doris to request Uncle Abe's autograph. Instead, she asked, "Can I get you some sweet tea, sugar? Maybe a few cookies?"

What a total attitude turnaround. Not that Imogene minded. This honeyed tone was much better than the previous vinegar in her voice. "No, thank you. I'm fine for now."

"Then I guess I'll just bring you a sweet sheikh." Doris guffawed all the way out the door, obviously quite impressed with her sense of humor.

Imogene tried to relax, but not as much as she had in the barn apartment the day before. Her face fired up when she thought about Raf Shakir coming in and catching her in the midst of one heck of a fantasy—about him. Surely he hadn't guessed. Even if he'd had his suspicions, he couldn't have known the details of her naughty thoughts.

"So you have decided to return."

Startled, Imogene glanced up to see him filling the doorway. The man was a total dichotomy in terms of his persona. One minute he appeared to be common, the next he could be a king. Right now he was dressed in his work attire—faded denim shirt and jeans. She couldn't decide which way she liked him best, sweating or sophisticated.

Imogene leaped to her feet and as lack of grace would have it, tripped over her suitcase and would have fallen on her face had he not rushed to right her, catching her in his substantial arms.

Of all the Hollywood cliché things to do. Imogene wouldn't be a bit surprised if he thought she'd planned the pratfall just so she could experience the mass of manliness pressed against her breasts.

"Sorry," she muttered. "I'm sure this probably has you doubting my abilities to handle a moving horse if I can't handle a motionless suitcase."

Oddly, he didn't let her go. "I cannot assess your abilities until I've had more time with you."

Imogene experienced a sudden lack of motivation to move away from him. But she had no choice in the matter when he framed her shoulders and steadied her, at the same time taking a step back.

He picked up her suitcases and said, "I will show you to your room."

She expected him to leave out the door and head toward the barn but instead, he made an immediate right out of the room and up the antebellum staircase. At the top landing, he took another right down a lengthy corridor sporting plush royal blue peacock-patterned carpet and myriad statues of gods and goddesses in various states of undress. This opulence indicated exactly who he was and what he owned, probably at least five fortunes.

The familiar decor was very similar to the accoutrements she'd grown up with—lots of antiques, charming, traditional, except when it came to the bedroom he indicated with a sweep of one large hand. "Your quarters for the duration."

Imogene stepped inside to further examine the room that

housed chic contemporary fixtures, from the chrome king-size bed and plush white carpet to the mirrored wall framing a black marble fireplace. On the far side of the room, an open door showcased a step-down Roman soaking tub flanked by white marble columns. To the right of that entry, a small ivory chaise sat next to the French doors leading onto the black wrought-iron-encased verandah overlooking the grounds. "This is wonderful," she said as she faced Raf. "But I'm a little surprised by the furnishings."

He looked concerned. "Is it not to your liking? There are several other rooms. Most were restored to their original state when I bought this house."

"This is fine. I'm more into ultramodern than antiques. Frilly doesn't suit my tastes."

Yet oddly enough, Imogene felt small and fragile in the room despite her average height and build. Must be the high ceilings and all the glass, she decided. Or it could be the tall, dark man standing in the center of the room that made the place—and Imogene—feel blatantly feminine. Regardless, the suite was comfortable and more than suitable for the time she would reside in his house. Of course, it might be fun to try out the sheikh's bed.

"My suite is two doors down," he said, as if channeling her thoughts. "Should you need anything during the night while you are here, you may call me on the intercom."

"I'm not sure what I would need from you at night." Actually, she knew exactly what she might need from him a night, not that she would ever ask.

"Perhaps some company."

That would be very tempting, but unprofessional. "I live alone. I'm used to solitude."

"And I am certain there are nights when you cannot sleep."

Now how in the devil did he know that? "Most nights I sleep fine."

"But others you do not. I, too, have trouble sleeping at times."

"I guess business has a way of intruding, even at night."

"Perhaps, but not always business."

As he studied her with his intense gray eyes, Imogene got the odd feeling that he knew exactly what disturbed her dreams. Or maybe she only wanted to know someone who understood, and that was just plain silly. She barely knew the man, although she would like to remedy that, and soon.

He set her bags on the floor at the foot of the bed. "You may change now and we will have our first lesson before lunch."

"Change into what?"

"Something more suitable."

Imogene glanced down at her black slacks, white sneakers and turquoise tank top. "What's wrong with what I have on?"

"Did you not bring any riding clothes?"

"Actually, no, since I don't own any."

Looking somewhat put out, he walked to the intercom near the door and said, "Doris, please bring Ms. Danforth some appropriate English riding attire."

"Alrighty, boss," Doris called back in her cheerful voice.

With one push of a button, just like that, he had anything he desired. Imogene figured that held true when it came to women, as well. And she would definitely like to have him push a few of her buttons.

"When you are ready, meet me in the stables," Raf said, then exited the room before Imogene could even manage a goodbye.

Raf Shakir was more an enigma than ever. Yesterday he displayed a few smiles and an easy charm; today he was aloof. Just what she needed, another moody man in her life. But only for three weeks.

Maybe that was for the best. After all, he wasn't really Imogene's type, if she could even peg her type. So far she hadn't met that elusive man who could appreciate her head for business and a heart she reserved for her loving family.

Maybe someday.

A few moments later, Doris entered the room clutching a pair of beige jodhpurs and a pair of black field boots. "Here, sugar. Try these on. They look like they should fit you. If you don't like the color, I have more."

"The color's fine." Imogene took the breeches and held them up. "Where did these come from?"

Doris averted her eyes. "Some woman."

"I gathered that."

"They didn't belong to Sheikh Shakir's wife, if that's what you're worried about."

Wife? "He's married?"

Doris's gaze snapped back to Imogene. "Not anymore. Didn't you find out anything about him before you agreed to move in here?"

"Only in terms of his horse business." And Imogene was already regretting that fact.

Doris shook her head. "I'm not at liberty to give you details about his past. And in case you get it in your head to ask any questions, the sheikh is a private man, so don't think you're going to get him to talk. Me, either."

Although Imogene was interested in finding out what exactly happened to Raf Shakir's wife, she thought it best not to ask too many questions if she wanted to earn the housekeeper's trust. Then maybe the facts would unfold naturally, without her coercion. "His personal life doesn't interest me."

Doris braced both hands on her generous hips. "Honey, if you're not interested in him on a personal level, then that would be a first. Most of the belles around here are dying to get to know him better."

"I gave up that whole 'belle' attitude years ago." Right after her required come-out, which she'd attended under duress. After that, she'd taken her bow and bowed out of the upwardly mobile scene, but soon discovered she couldn't escape that atmosphere in her line of work. She'd grown up with money. She made her own money from people with money. But as they said, riches couldn't buy that elusive happiness. They also couldn't find a missing young woman.

Imogene sat on the edge of the bed and toed out of her sneakers. "Tell me, Doris, have any of the 'belles' succeeded in knowing the sheikh better?" She regretted the question immediately when she saw the sly look Doris sent her.

"He's a man, sugar. And all the men I've known have to take care of things now and again, else they'll explode." Doris followed with her trademark cackle.

"Then you're saying he doesn't have a steady girlfriend?" Imogene cringed at the hint of hope in her tone.

This time Doris gave her a knowing look. "Land sakes, child, are you interested in the royal goods?"

How stupid to be so obvious to a wise old owl like Doris. "Actually, no. I'm just curious. I want to make sure that I'm not confronted by some jealous woman who doesn't appreciate me living here."

"That won't happen, sugar. He's been in a drought for a while."

Imogene almost laughed considering that's exactly how she'd termed her romantic life. "I'm only interested in learning to ride."

Doris winked. "Oh, the sheikh will be an expert teacher. And he'll eventually teach you how to ride a horse, too."

With that, the housekeeper left out the door on a flurry of more grating giggles and the scent of overpowering lavender perfume.

Imogene slipped her pants off and wriggled into the jodh-purs and boots. She stood in front of the mirrored wall, pleased to find that everything fit, yet somehow discon-certed by the fact she was wearing another woman's clothes. Probably one of his lover's clothes.

If that were true, then why would Raf Shakir hang on to them? Did he see them as a souvenir of a relationship that had been memorable before it had gone sour? Memories of a woman he still pined for? That wouldn't surprise Imogene in the least. Maybe he'd had a lover who had left him high and dry. Or had he been the one to do the leaving?

That seemed more logical to Imogene. The ''handsome confident man who wanted no ties, no commitments'' sit-uation. Yes, Raf Shakir was probably the love 'em and leave 'em kind. The kind of man who should be avoided like a bad investment.

Of course, she couldn't entirely avoid him, considering she was putting her tutelage in his capable hands. And she needed to remember to keep everything else away from those hands. But, oh, how easy it would be to forget.

The minute his ''apprentice'' appeared in the stable, Raf wanted to put his hands all over her. The jodhpurs empha-sized her long legs, the pleasing curve of her thighs and hips. He silently offered up his gratitude to the very de-ceitful Mary Christine Chatham for leaving the clothes in her haste and anger when he had not accepted her marriage proposal. She had been twice insulted when he had not accepted her offer of sex, either. Yet he doubted she had missed the garments as much as she had mourned the lost opportunity to snag a wealthy husband.

Raf had to admit the clothing looked better on Genie, and that could prove detrimental to his concentration. Per-haps he had subconsciously subjected himself to the sweetest kind of torture, knowing they would highlight the finer aspects of her body. Or perhaps he was testing his strength of will. However, he was destined to fail if he did not stop staring at her or imagining what it would be like to touch her beneath that clothing.

Gathering his resolve, Raf motioned for Genie to come forward. "I have someone I would like you to meet."

She took a few tentative steps. "The *real* stable boy?"

"No, but he is male and quite friendly."

She finally joined him at the stall and peered inside, her eyes wide. "My gosh, he dwarfs that saddle! Am I really supposed to ride something that big?"

The gelding would definitely not be considered above average height, at least to someone accustomed to horses. "I am assuming that your last experience involved a pony."

She looked chagrined. "It was a big pony."

He tried to hide a smile, without success, but he only allowed it for a moment. "He is trustworthy."

She folded her arms beneath her breasts. "I hope so."

Raf opened the stall door and the gelding continued to gorge on hay without acknowledging his visitors. "I have a lady who has come to see you, Maurice."

Genie released a terse laugh. "Maurice? You have a horse named Maurice?"

"Maurice is strictly his barn name, given to him by his previous owner who named him after her late husband. His official name is King Jassim sháaTir of miSir, if you prefer to call him that."

She shrugged. "Maurice it is."

When she failed to move forward, Raf took her by the hand and led her into the stall, relishing the feel of her slender fingers entwined with his. "You must get acquainted with him now." And perhaps Raf would become better acquainted with her soon. All of her.

Before he disregarded the reasons for their liaison, Raf

released his grasp on her hand, took her by the shoulders and guided her forward.

When the gelding turned and sniffed, Genie stood as stiff as the metal structure surrounding them. "Hey, Maurice. How's it going?"

The horse lowered his head and plucked a single straw from the floor before approaching her to nuzzle her palm, most likely searching for a treat. Genie continued to stand still, looking somewhat wary.

"Do not be afraid to touch him," Raf said. "He is gentle."

She finally raised one hand to scratch the gelding behind his ears, prompting Maurice to press his muzzle between her breasts. Raf envied the beast at that moment and felt the beginnings of sexual stirrings. He silently cursed his absence of control over his base urges, knowing this was only the beginning of his struggle.

"He's just a big baby," Genie said, her expression reflecting delight over the horse's attention.

"He prefers women to men. He always has, regardless that he can no longer breed."

Genie turned her gaze from Maurice to Raf. "That seems totally unfair. How's he supposed to have any fun?"

"He greatly enjoys taking occasional trips along the trails that lead to the water. That is the extent of his activities." Very much like Raf's existence of late, only he had chosen to keep his solitude when it came to his personal life. He had intentionally concentrated on tending his prize horses, building his business and reputation in America in order to block out the past. Some days that worked well. Others it did not. On rare occasions, he had escorted various women, but only to public functions for appearance's sake. No woman had completely captured his interest...until now.

In Genie's presence, he experienced an unfamiliar longing to know once more the rewards of keeping company with a woman for more than an evening. How strange that she should uncover that desire within him after such a brief time. Perhaps it was only primal lust. Perhaps it was her strength of will. Perhaps it was simply the joy in her face, the childlike innocence, as she discovered an affinity with an animal.

She tipped her forehead against Maurice's forehead as a mother might do to a child. "Okay, big guy. You take care of me, I'll take care of you. If you promise me that, I'm sure I can talk your master out of something better to eat than those dry oats."

Raf withdrew a piece of candy from his pocket. "You may give him this."

Genie stared at his hand. "He likes peppermints?"

"Yes." He took her hand and opened it to place the treat in the well of her palm. "Be certain to hold your hand flat and allow him to take it from you. He is good-natured, but he does become eager when it comes to food."

Genie did as he'd asked, pleasing Raf to know that she did follow instructions. After Maurice consumed the candy, Raf hooked the *longe* line to the bridle. "Now we shall begin your first lesson."

She stepped out of the stall first and Raf followed, pulling a reluctant Maurice behind him as he admired the bow of Genie's hips, the narrow waist, the roundness of her bottom that would fit nicely in his palms.

"Where are we going?" she asked.

If he had his way, to his bed. "To the outdoor arena. We will start out slowly, then work our way up to more difficult tasks."

She turned to face him, walking backward as they continued to the exit. Although he could no longer view her bottom, he did have a good view of her breasts. "How slowly are we going to take it?"

As slowly as she desired. All night, until dawn. Until they were both replete. "We will start out slowly, with walking only. We will progress beyond that when I feel you are ready."

"That sounds kind of boring."

As suspected, she would not be easy to control. That would bode well for lovemaking, but not for lessons. "Perhaps it does seem unexciting, but it is necessary."

"I'm a quick study."

"There are many things you must know about horses, and much to learn about how to show them what you want." The same as it was between a man and a woman. The way it would be between him and Genie, if he decided to take that course.

"I guess horses have to learn to read your signals," she said. "Your body language."

Her body was speaking to Raf on a very primitive level. "Precisely. They must learn the proper cues."

She moved to his side. "One wrong signal and they might assume the wrong thing."

"Yes."

"Certain cues mean go, others mean stop."

"I will show you."

"Good. I wouldn't want to make any wrong moves or mistake something for what it wasn't at all."

He looked from the path leading to the arena to her luminous smile. "You will know all the correct cues, I assure you."

"But we still have to take our time?"

He paused at the gate leading to the arena and faced her. "Yes. Slowly. Until I know you feel certain of your abilities. Until you feel confident."

"Good. I'm looking forward to it." She swept one hand through her hair, golden highlights reflecting the June sun. "But just so you know, I have a lot of confidence in my abilities. And it doesn't take me very long to learn, if I want something badly enough.''

The challenge in her eyes acted on Raf like a potent poison, flowing through his veins and settling in his loins. "How badly do you want this?"

"If I didn't want it badly, I wouldn't be here, now, would I?"

How simple it would be to release the gelding and take this woman into his arms. Maurice would not wander far, but Raf feared he would go too far, too fast. They were in the open and several of his men were taking in the scene from the breeding stables in the immediate area. They would know simply by looking at his face that he wanted Genie. Fiercely, without hesitation. Yet his reasons for keeping his distance won out, for now.

He opened the gate and told her, "Go inside." His tone was harsher than he'd intended, but he was driven by a desire as untamed as the wilds in the distance.

After he tethered Maurice to the fencing, Raf gestured to Genie once more. "You may climb on now."

"On the horse?"

He considered several responses to that query. "What else would I be referring to?"

Her cheeks turned a light shade of pink. "Of course the horse. What else?" She surveyed the saddle. "But I'm not sure I can get up there all by myself. Mind giving me a boost?"

A request Raf had feared. Yet he did recognize that she would need some assistance, considering the tight fit of the breeches.

"Lift your leg and place your foot into the irons," he told her when she faced the horse.

She regarded him over one shoulder. "Irons?"

"The stirrup."

With some effort, she complied. "Okay. I'm ready."

So was Raf. Ready to turn and leave the premises before he pulled her away from the horse and carried her to his bed. Instead, he molded her bottom with his palm, lingering there longer than necessary before he pushed her up onto the saddle.

She looked down on him and said, "Now that wasn't so hard."

Oh, but it was. Harder than she realized. "You must keep your shoulders and body straight, elbows at your sides." He fashioned her hands around the reins. "Maintain a light grip."

She tipped up her chin and straightened. "Like this?"

Although her position might be deemed adequate, Raf laid one palm on her lower back, the other on her abdomen above the waistband of the jodhpurs, imagining what it would be like to slip beneath the fabric. Instead, he only applied enough pressure to tighten her frame. "Like this."

"Okay, what now?"

"Keep your eyes focused ahead, hold on with your legs and knees, toes pointed out, heels close to his sides."

"That's a lot to remember."

"In time, it will come naturally for you."

Yet when Raf took his place in the center of the pen, controlling Maurice with the line attached to his bridle, he noted that Genie looked very natural in the saddle, and very beautiful. She appeared to be concentrating, allowing Raf the opportunity to study her features. Her breasts were high, round, and he wondered over the color of her nipples. He suspected they were a pale shade of pink. Or perhaps the tones found in a coral sunset. Regardless, he knew exactly how they would feel to his hand, how they would taste in his mouth, against his tongue. With every imagining, he hardened more, again cursing his lack of control and good judgment.

After only a few rounds, he halted Maurice and brought him into the center of the pen. "That is all for now."

Her face showed her displeasure. "That's it?"

"Yes. We will begin again after lunch. You may come down now."

"Mind helping me?"

He did not dare. "I believe you can do it yourself."

She leaned over and looked at the ground. "It's a long way down."

"Bring your leg over the saddle and work your way off."

"Show me."

"You seem to be quite capable."

"Maybe, but I could use some help the first time."

Driven by a need to feel her against him, he tossed the line aside and pulled her from the saddle, sliding her slowly down his body, creating flashes of heat at each point they touched. He held her securely in his arms, her breasts against his chest, her thighs molding to his thighs, her pelvis contacting his building erection. If she had not known what she was doing to him before, she most certainly did now.

"Now that's service," she said, her gaze locked into his eyes as firmly as her body fitted to his body.

How easy it would be to take her mouth. How easy to learn how she would taste when his kissed her. He would only have to lower his head and know…

A whistle coming from behind him caused Raf to drop his arms from around her and take a much-needed step back. "I will deliver Maurice to one of the workers to be rinsed off. You may go into the house now. Doris has prepared lunch."

She frowned. "Can I help give him his bath?"

Raf almost requested her assistance with his own bath. "Perhaps at a later time."

"Okay. But this seemed like a very short lesson. I'm not sure I got my money's worth today."

"You will be duly rewarded as long as you practice patience."

"Another part of the Sheikh Shakir Slow-Moving Method?"

"Yes."

"I'll agree to that." She presented a bright smile. "For now."

"You will not be sorry."

She sent a direct look at his fly, indicating she had noticed his predicament. "I guess that remains to be seen."

Genie turned on her booted heels and swayed toward the house, leaving Raf alone with a lethargic horse and a need greater than he'd predicted.

He would make certain she would have no regrets. And he would do well to remember his own vow of patience. Still, he would have her if she came willingly to his bed, but only when the time was right.

After all, he had waited two years for this opportunity. He could certainly wait a few more days.

Three

———

"**T**hanks for the lunch, Doris," Imogene called out as she pushed back from the table after eating alone. Of course, Doris had made an appearance into the small dining room a few times to check on Imogene, but that didn't exactly qualify as good company, especially when she'd let go a string of curses after letting the pot of chicken soup boil over. Having lunch with Raf might have been nicer, had he shown up for the meal. But since their lesson, she hadn't seen him at all. And she wasn't even sure when he wanted her to return for the next round of instructions.

Doris came in from the kitchen, wiping her hands on a dish towel and immediately homed in on the half-eaten bowl of soup. "Didn't you like it, honey? Or was it too spicy?"

Spicy wouldn't begin to describe the three-alarm concoction. "It was great but I didn't want to get too full before my afternoon lesson." She hooked a thumb over her shoulder. "I guess I should see if Sheikh Shakir is ready now."

Doris grinned. "I'm sure he is." Her smile dropped into a frown. "But you're not. If you don't put something on that skin of yours, you're going to blister like a crawfish in boiling water."

What a lovely visual, Imogene in the role of cooked shellfish. "I've already put on some sunscreen."

"Are you sure you have on enough? I'd hate to have to get out the vinegar for you to bathe in. My boss doesn't appreciate that smell."

With great effort, Imogene quelled a comeback about how she didn't really care about how she smelled to the sheikh, when in fact that was a lie. She'd cared enough to take a quick shower the minute she'd returned to the house. "I'll make sure I have on enough sunblock to prevent that from happening."

As Imogene headed for the kitchen's back door, Doris called out, "Be sure you put some more on after you sweat it off, sugar. And after you have your lesson, too."

The sound of Doris's raucous laughter followed Imogene all the way out the exit and down the path leading to the stables. Why did the housekeeper continue to misread her motives where Raf was concerned? It wasn't as if Imogene had "I want him" written all over her face. Or did she?

From now on, she would be extra careful when it came to talking about Raf. In fact, she probably shouldn't talk about him at all in front of Doris, if she could stop Doris from talking about him herself. She'd probably find monkeys grazing in the pasture before that happened.

Imogene walked into the stable where she'd found Raf earlier only to discover the place empty except for several horses occupying the stalls. Snorting, restless horses that she presumed to be stallions. She kept her distance as she made her way to Maurice's stall, finding it vacant, too.

Deciding that Raf could already have Maurice ready for the next lesson, Imogene left the barn and walked the path to the arena to find she'd been right. Maurice was tied to the rail near the gate, but he wasn't saddled. He also wasn't alone.

Raf Shakir rode along the inside perimeter of the pen on an exquisite stallion fitted with an unadorned western work saddle that had seen better days. The prince wore no flowing robes or golden crowns to indicate he'd been born into royalty, just a pair of scuffed boots and the same faded jeans—and no shirt. He could be any typical cowboy out for a day on the trail, but he wasn't, as far as Imogene was concerned. Breathtaking, yes. Typical, no.

One beautiful man with raven hair blowing back in the breeze and one dutiful beast with an equally black coat and mane galloped in perfect synchronization. The horse's and rider's muscles bunched, their tendons flexed, both absorbed in the moment as if blocking out the world.

Imogene climbed up three fence rungs at the north side of the arena to get a firsthand view of the remarkable scene playing out before her, content to watch the ultimate portrait of power as they rode away from her. She remained undetected until Raf rounded the pen and headed in her direction. When he reached her observation point, he pulled the stallion to a halt and pinned Imogene in place with extreme gray eyes that contrasted with the bright sunlight. His bare chest, glistening with sweat, rose and fell with labored breaths. The horse's coat and respiration also showed the signs of exertion. Obviously both studs had been through quite a workout.

"You're a great rider," Imogene said despite the fact that his continued perusal and silence disconcerted her. And so did his state of undress, exactly as it had yesterday in the stable. She struggled to keep from staring at all the aspects that made him unequivocally male—the breadth of his chest, the strength of his shoulders, the flat plane of his abdomen and below that the prominent ridge that removed all doubt about his chromosomes. Like there would ever be any doubt. The man could be the model for a testosterone ad.

Without taking his gaze from Imogene's face, Raf slipped his feet from the stirrups to let his long legs dangle, leaned forward and stroked the horse's neck. "This is Layl BáHar and, when translated into English means 'black sea.' I call him BáHar. No one is allowed to touch him but me."

His possessive tone sent a little shiver up Imogene's stiff spine, not because of fear. Because she was hit with the fantasy of him declaring the same thing about her. How ridiculously archaic was that?

"Beautiful," she said, referring to both the man and the horse.

"Are you ready?" he asked, his voice low with a noticeable edge.

If not careful, Imogene could very well dissolve from the heat of the sun and his lethal gaze. "Ready for what?"

"To ride."

"The horse?"

"For now."

"I'm ready when you are."

"I have been ready for a while now."

So had Imogene, but not for her lesson. She was ready to forget why she was here. Forget business altogether. She couldn't do that. Too much was at stake. Too much to lose.

Like a well-oiled manly machine, Raf dismounted with ease and left the reins loosely looped around the saddle horn, issuing a command to the horse that Imogene couldn't understand. The stallion obediently remained in place, not making any effort to move aside from the occasional swish of his tail.

Imogene understood all too well Raf Shakir's magnetism. She, too, failed to move when he passed by her and left the arena to retrieve Maurice, even when a fly flitted about her face and nose, threatening to send her into another sneezing fit until she finally batted it away.

Raf came back with Maurice and told her, "I will hold him while you mount."

Imogene's mouth dropped open. "Where's the saddle?"

"This afternoon, you will ride bareback."

No way could she do that. "I won't have anything to hold on to if I lose my balance."

"You will learn to balance better."

"I really don't think this is a good idea."

He rounded Maurice and stood by the horse's side. "I will ride along with you and make certain you do not fall."

That sounded like a banner idea, but she didn't want him to think she was a total ninny. "I'm not sure *that's* necessary." She didn't sound at all confident.

"Our agreement stated that you would abide by my instructions," he said, a trace of impatience in his tone.

Imogene absently scratched Maurice's nose as she inclined her head to stare at the dictator. "I'm willing to follow instructions unless I think they might kill me."

He gave her one heck of a fierce glare, almost frightening in its intensity. "I will not let any harm come to you if you do what I say, and you must do what I say. Is that understood?"

Imogene saluted with her free hand and clicked her heels together. "Yes, sir. I apologize for being so impertinent, sir."

Raf rubbed his hands on his solid, denim-covered thighs, drawing Imogene's immediate attention. She forced herself to watch him from the waist up while he brought BáHar to Maurice's side. Maurice snorted and tried to nip at the stallion as if incensed that another animal might be receiving more attention.

Great. A horse fight. And poor Maurice, unlike BáHar, had been robbed of his male equipment, which could put him at a disadvantage. As good luck would have it, BáHar ignored Maurice's attempts at sniping and continued to stand as still as an equine statue.

"Come here," Raf commanded, and it took Imogene a moment to recognize he was addressing her and not the horse. Before she could prepare, he moved behind her, very closely and said in a deep, drugging voice, "Hold the reins and I will help you up."

As soon as she answered his request, he grabbed her bottom and hoisted her onto Maurice's somewhat concave back. Imogene felt totally helpless with no stirrups for her feet and only Maurice's bony back beneath her butt. She felt even more helpless when she looked down at Raf and found him staring at her breasts. Under his scrutiny, her nipples hardened against her sports bra. Not enough material existed to cover the evidence and she certainly couldn't blame it on the weather, considering it had to be over eighty degrees.

Then sun beat down on her bare shoulders and she remembered she had not followed Doris's directive about applying more sunscreen. But a sunburn was the least of her concern. She was completely focused on Raf who had yet to move, his eyes now trained on her face.

"First, you will make one round alone while I watch," he said.

Imogene tried to keep her panic reined in while white-knuckling the reins. "Alone?"

"I will be right here. Urge Maurice forward by pumping your legs," he said. "Slowly."

Imogene did and after some effort, Maurice took three steps then stopped dead, throwing Imogene forward where she grabbed his neck as her nose crushed into his mane. Appropriately, she sneezed.

After righting herself, she discovered Raf was right there, his hands coming around her waist when she listed to one side. "This is not going to work," she said. "I feel like I'm on a slippery slide, not a horse."

He studied her for a long moment but Imogene saw only concern and contemplation in his expression, not anger or judgment. "I have a better idea," he told her then pulled her off of Maurice, easy as you please.

Imogene had a better idea, too, when she came face-to-face with his bare chest. "What do you have in mind?" she muttered as she fought the urge to test the taste of his skin with the tip of her tongue.

Without elaborating on the idea, he stepped away, yanked off BáHar's saddle, tossed it over the top rail of the fence as if it were a rag, then mounted the stallion with little effort. He signaled a man who was coming out of the nearby stable with a whistle. "Blaylock, return Maurice to his stall. We are finished with him for the day."

The silver-haired man called out, "Yes, sir," then rushed into the pen and led Maurice out of the arena, all the while keeping his eyes lowered as if he were disturbing something very intimate. If only he were right, Imogene thought as she stared up at Raf, sitting proudly on BáHar's broad back, looking like some desert god.

"Come closer," he told her in that voice that made her want to fall to her knees and worship his sheer sensuality.

On noodle legs, Imogene complied, shocked into silence when he reached down and snatched her from the ground as if she weighed no more than a very small sack of cornmeal. He positioned her in front of him and snaked his arm around her midriff, pulling her close until her back pressed against his front. She was all too aware of his thighs touching her thighs, his sandalwood scent and his overwhelming heat.

"You just took about ten years off my life with that trick," Imogene said.

"This will give you the opportunity to learn the way a horse feels beneath you. And I will be here to guide you."

"I thought you said no one could touch him but you."

"For you I will make an exception." He slid his palms down her bare arms. "Take the reins in your hands as I showed you and attempt to relax. He will sense if you are nervous."

"I am nervous." And very needy in a not so bad way.

His warm breath played across her ear when he said, "You have no reason to be nervous. I am here to protect you. To teach you."

Imogene did as he asked, holding the leather in both hands as he'd shown her earlier. Frankly, right now, she would do anything he asked. "Is this okay?"

"Yes. Now hold on tightly with your legs."

Her muscles felt like mush, loose and uncooperative.

Raf slid his free hand down the side of her left thigh. "More. Harder."

When she envisioned saying the same thing to him during lovemaking, her heart pounded like a bongo in her chest. She tried to ignore Raf's hand on her thigh and concentrate on his directive, squeezing her legs against Bá-Har's sides. Against the heat gathering between them.

"That is better," he said. "Tap your heels slightly to cue him to move forward."

Remarkably, the horse answered her silent signal without hesitation, unlike Maurice, and took a few easy steps before picking up the pace, as if he really wanted to run.

"Talk to him," Raf murmured. "That will slow him."

"What am I supposed to say?"

"He responds to the word *easy*."

Imogene stared down on the horse's ears that twitched as if he waited for her command. "Easy."

"Say it more firmly."

"Easy," Imogene repeated, a little louder this time and amazingly, it worked.

They walked around the pen at a relaxed gait although Imogene couldn't claim she was all that relaxed. She wanted to lean back against Raf and close her eyes, enjoy the feel of him against her. Instead, she reluctantly tried to focus on the lesson.

"What now?" she asked.

"We will continue this way until you feel comfortable before we progress."

"Am I ever going to do something other than walk?"

"When you are ready."

Her breath caught in her chest when Raf's right hand slid down from her middle to her abdomen where he lightly stroked the terrain with his thumb. "Relax your hips and follow the horse's movement."

Imogene could only follow the movement of his fingertips stroking her belly. "Okay."

"If you wish to stop, then you must pull lightly on the reins. He has a very sensitive mouth."

"A sensitive mouth, huh?" She looked back over her shoulder, their faces so close she could see every detail of Raf's incredible lips. With little difficulty, she could even kiss him.

"You should try it," he said.

He was giving her permission? "I should?"

"You will see how simple it is to stop him."

Darn. He'd meant the horse.

Imogene pulled back on the reins and the stallion stopped. She cued him forward and he answered. She stopped him again then cued him forward again. "He's very well trained," she said. "Much more cooperative than Maurice today."

"You are doing well, Genie," Raf whispered. "Very well."

Unable to stop herself, Imogene leaned her head back against his shoulder. "Am I?" She sounded sluggish. She felt sluggish, boneless.

His cheek rested against hers as he worked his fingertips beneath the hem of her blouse, contacting her bare flesh. "You are catching on quickly."

"Then why are we only walking?" And why was she starting to tremble? Dumb question. Raf's touch made her shiver, made her want.

He traced the edge of the waistband of her breeches with a lazy fingertip, back and forth in a mind-melting rhythm. "As I've said, we are taking it slowly."

"I see." And she did see. She could also feel and want all those things she had put on the back burner because of her career. She longed for him to keep touching her, to soothe the ache that had everything to do with desire for a man. This man.

Raf continued to draw random designs on her stomach, breezing a fingertip right below the waistband, lower with each stroke. Her breath hitched painfully in her chest when she felt him toy with the clasp. Of course, she should put an end to this before he went any farther. She really should ask him what he was doing. She shouldn't want him to continue, but she did.

Abruptly he pulled his hand from beneath her blouse then the reins from her grasp. He brought BáHar to a stop before the gate and dismounted.

Imogene stared at him from her perch on the horse. "That's it?" Her tone carried the weight of her disappointment and frustration.

"Enough for one day."

He clasped Imogene's waist and pulled her from the

horse, this time setting her aside before leading the stallion out of the pen without even a backward glance.

Imogene stood in the same spot for a time, annoyance seeping through her pores like the perspiration that had formed on her back where Raf's body had met hers. Annoyance because she still wanted him. Regret because she hadn't wanted it to end. And worse, he knew it. He also knew exactly what he was doing to her and what she wanted him to do. But he was determined to withhold his affections. Determined to seduce her into senselessness. And damn him, it was working.

Quickening her pace, she caught up with Raf in the barn as he handed the horse off to the man named Blaylock and told him, "Take BáHar and bathe him. Give him extra hay as a reward." The man hurried away with the horse without uttering a word. Obviously everyone bowed to Raf Shakir's every whim. If she wasn't careful, she would find herself among them.

Imogene leaned her shoulder against one stall while Raf took his shirt from the top of a grooming cart and slipped it on. "Don't I get some kind of reward for being a good student?"

He faced her with a smile that caught her totally off guard. "Actually, I have something to show you."

That sounded very promising. "What might that be?"

He nodded toward the stairs leading to the apartment. "Come with me."

Imogene wanted to skip behind him like a child, knowing that they would probably be alone. As she followed him up the stairs, once more she took in all the wonderful details of his body, and particularly his jean-clad butt.

He opened the door and allowed her inside first, then locked them in. Imogene chafed her arms, immediately noting a slight sting but she honestly didn't care. She was much too keyed up to find out what the sheikh had in mind to worry about the beginnings of a sunburn.

Raf opened the French doors to the office. "I want to discuss with you the business deal I mentioned earlier."

He wanted to talk business? Of course. After all, that's why she was here, what they both wanted. It did disappoint her, though, and she hated her sudden lack of good sense.

Imogene hesitated for a moment before she strolled into the office and took her place in front of the desk while Raf stood behind it. He opened a folder and slid it before her. "This is a list of interested parties who would be willing to buy shares in BáHar. They will split the proceeds from his breeding income if they participate. They will also share in the expense and be allotted two free breedings per year, as long as they bring high-quality mares."

She studied the names that looked like a list of Who's Who in Georgia society. "I recognize a few of these people. They all have big bucks. How much will they have to invest?"

"Each share will cost thirty thousand dollars. I intend to sell only twenty."

"He's worth that much?"

"More. I will retain my own shares as well."

"That sounds reasonable, but I've never been involved with anything like this before." She'd never been involved with anyone like him before, either. She felt uncharacteristically insecure on both counts. "Maybe you should ask someone who has done this kind of thing."

"I trust your judgment. And I would be willing to let your institution handle the details and the funds."

That would thrill Sid to death. She raised her eyes from the folder and contacted his unwavering gaze. "Just like that?"

"Yes. I believe you've earned the opportunity."

Wow. What a boon. She'd already earned Raf's business

and she didn't even have to sleep with him. Darn it. "Okay. We can discuss the particulars while I'm here. And unless you're in a big hurry, I can set everything up next month, after I'm finished with my lessons and I return to work." Work. What a foul word.

Raf leaned over, palms braced on the desk, his open shirt giving Imogene an up-close view of his chest and flat belly. "As I've said, I am rarely in a hurry. Some endeavors are better served with patience."

"I guess that's best when it comes to the corporate world and riding lessons."

His eyes seemed to fade into black right before Imogene's eyes, prompting her pulse to race. "Other things are meant to be savored as well."

She shivered, but only slightly. "What other things?"

"Those not having to do with business."

Driven by a total lack of logic, Imogene leaned over the desk, as well, their hands almost touching, their faces only inches apart. "You know, I could use a few examples for clarity's sake."

"Are you certain?"

"Yes, I am."

Circling her nape with one hand, he pulled her head closer and touched his lips to her brow. "This." He kissed her cheek softly. "This." He kissed each corner of her mouth. "And this."

Imogene decided it was a start. A really nice start. But he wasn't finished. Not even close.

This time he inclined his head and kissed her full on the mouth, making gentle, teasing passes with his tongue between her parted lips. Imogene experienced a wave of heat that started in her breasts and billowed all the way down to her knees, gathering like an electrical storm in intimate places. She wanted his arms around her, his body pressed against hers. She wanted to feel the dampness of his skin and the muscles against her palms as she ran them over his chest. She wanted the damn desk gone.

He increased the pressure with his mouth, deepened the kiss but only slightly. Yet it was enough to have Imogene considering climbing over the furniture and tackling him. Before she could do that, he ended the kiss and straightened.

"Doris serves dinner at seven," he said in a surprisingly formal tone considering their recent informal behavior. "I suggest you not be late, otherwise she will not serve you."

Dinner? Imogene pushed back from the desk and straightened her shirt, more out of nervousness than need. "So that's it?"

"Yes, since I do not know until I sit at the table what she will be serving."

"I'm not referring to dinner."

"I know." He turned away but not before Imogene caught a glimpse of his smile.

Blast him. "You're going to walk out of here now, like nothing ever happened between us?"

He faced her again, his fingers clutching the door handle. "What do you believe happened between us, Genie?"

"You kissed me and quite thoroughly, I might add."

"And I am certain it will not be the last time."

"You sound pretty confident about that."

"I am. And you know it will happen again, as well."

The man had way too much confidence—and charisma. "What if I don't want it to happen again?"

His eyes narrowed and a self-assured smile curled the corners of his sensuous mouth. "You have no choice."

Of all the chauvinistic comments. "I have no choice? Isn't that a little bit of an antiquated attitude? After all, this is the twenty-first century and I am entitled to my own choices and the say-so in regard to my own needs." She paused only to draw a quick breath. "In fact, I am quite in tune with my sexuality and what I want from a man and when and how I—''

He cut off her words with another kiss, this one so searing that Imogene was certain her straight hair had curled. Her body certainly had, right into his body where she could feel his strength, his heat, his hardness. All of it, including that ''happy'' part pressing against her pelvis when he cupped her bottom in his palms and nudged her forward. Sheikh Raf Shakir's mouth was as intoxicating as pricey champagne, going straight to Imogene's head until she truly thought she would to start swaying if he wasn't holding her so tightly. But all too soon he pulled away again.

Imogene pushed her hair from her face and tucked it behind her ears. ''I suppose you did that to prove a point?''

''Actually, I have come to the conclusion that occupying your mouth could be the only means to silence you.''

''And you think that's going to discourage me from speaking my mind?''

''No. But I will continue to silence you however I see fit.''

Overcome with determination, Imogene ran a fingertip from his sternum to his navel, feeling his muscles clench beneath her touch. ''I do believe the sheikh is not as in control as he pretends to be.''

He caught her hand in his, turned it over and lifted her palm to his mouth for a kiss that ended with his tongue sliding over her wrist. ''I can be very controlled, Genie, when I, too, want something badly enough.''

Imogene did not want to feel hot. She did not want to feel excited. But darned if she wasn't both. ''What is it that you want, Raf?''

''You.''

That one word trapped her breath and sent her heart into a tailspin. ''And you think you're going to have me, do you?''

"Yes. Eventually. But we will go slowly."

She really wanted hard and fast. "Slowly?"

"Yes. And I assure you it will be well worth your wait. And mine."

Raf left the room while Imogene lost the last of her composure and her ability to remain upright. She collapsed into the chair in the corner and released a shaky breath. He was going to make her wait, but for how long? Would it be wise for her to take the risk? And if she did, would it be worth it?

Oh, yeah. Imogene had no doubt about that. As long as she remembered they were two very different people who happened to be experiencing a little chemistry.

A little chemistry? She honestly thought she might explode every time he looked at her. But she had a busy life that didn't include a serious relationship with a man—even a gorgeous one—at this point in time. If they did happen to explore their mutual attraction, she would keep a tight grip on her control.

Raf was doubtful he could hold on to his control much longer. Yesterday in the apartment, Imogene Danforth had affected him more than any woman in years. Today during her lessons, she had distracted him on several occasions. And now, even watching her doing ordinary things such as sipping her water while waiting for their dinner, he could not ignore her.

Although he had wanted to carry Genie to the apartment's bedroom several times today, he had managed to restrain himself. But now, if circumstances were different, if they were alone and undisturbed, he would gladly pull her from her chair, take her out onto the nearby verandah and make love to her under the stars.

"Chow's here," Doris announced as she set a plate before Raf and a large steaming bowl before Imogene, who looked as though Doris had served her a treasure trove.

Genie's eyes widened with pleasure. "Low Country Boil. How did you know that's my favorite?"

Doris patted her back. "Sugar, good Georgia gals appreciate the South's delicacies." She sent Raf an acrimonious look. "Some transplants don't."

Raf nodded. "I appreciate you accommodating my questionable tastes, Doris."

She addressed Imogene without giving Raf a second glance. "He's picky. He likes chicken and this stew I make for him all the time. The same old thing, day in and day out. I can't even get him to eat corn bread, if you can imagine that."

Genie laid a hand above her breast and feigned shock. "That's pure blasphemy. Who doesn't like corn bread?"

"I, for one," Raf stated and concentrated on cutting his overly dry poultry. He would not be surprised if Doris had left the dish in the oven too long to prove her point.

Doris strolled past Raf and patted his back. "You two enjoy. I've left you plenty of napkins, Miss Danforth. I expect you to use every one."

"Believe me, I will," Genie said, followed by a laugh. "She's a riot, Raf. You're lucky to have her."

At times he would disagree. Right now he wished Doris would take her leave into the next county so that Raf could be alone with Genie. "She is a very hard worker, although I do question her cooking."

"I heard that," came from the direction of the kitchen.

"She also has the ability to hear from twenty meters away," he muttered.

Genie stuffed a napkin in the front of her coral blouse and proceeded to pick up a prawn. "Would you like one?" she offered.

He studied it with disdain. "I am not fond of shellfish."

With slow movements, Genie held up the shrimp and peeled it, sparking Raf's thoughts of peeling away her clothes. "Are you sure? They're really good."

"I will have to trust you on that since I have no desire to try them." Raf did have an overpowering urge to sample her, however. He tried to concentrate on his own food, taking a bite yet tasting nothing even though Doris, as usual, had coated the chicken with heavy spices. He was more interested in watching Imogene partake of her food as she dipped the prawn into the rich butter sauce accompanying the dish, inched the morsel into her mouth then licked the butter off her lower lip. Raf wished he could do the same. He could, but he did not dare. Doris was no doubt lurking around the corner, waiting to see if she would catch him doing something he should not, in her opinion, be doing.

"This is great," Genie said with the enthusiasm Raf hoped to see when he finally did make love with her. And he would. Soon.

"I am glad to know you are enjoying yourself," he said. He would eventually show her more enjoyment in ways she had only imagined.

Again she peeled another shrimp, even slower this time. "Like you've said, some things are meant to be savored."

Raf kept his attention on his own food although he did manage a glance at her now and then. Yet every time she licked her lips, licked her fingers, he grew exceedingly hard beneath the napkin positioned in his lap.

"Did you find your accommodations satisfactory last night?" he asked.

"Yes. The bed's very comfortable. I was so tired I don't think a freight train running through the room would have woken me."

"I am glad to know that."

She dabbed at her mouth with a napkin. "It did get a

little warm, though. I ended up completely tangled up in the sheets, those that I didn't kick off onto the floor.''

Raf considered how she would look in tangled sheets and he, too, grew very warm. "The thermostat is in the hall should you need to adjust the temperature.''

"That's good to know, otherwise I might have to sleep naked.''

If he did not leave soon, Raf was in grave danger of losing his dignity and his resolve to take this slowly. After pushing his chair away from the table, Raf stood. "I am retiring for the evening. Good night.''

Genie stared up at him. "I thought maybe we might take some time to talk about your syndication ideas.''

If he remained in her presence much longer, there would be no talking. "You should rest. I expect you to be at the stables by eight o'clock tomorrow morning.''

"Fine. I'll be there.''

"And you should wear long sleeves.''

"It's too hot for that.''

Raf was too hot. "Your skin has reddened, worse than yesterday.''

She held out her arms. "It's only a minor burn. In a few days it will turn into a tan. It always does.'' She raised her gaze to him. "Not all of us are blessed with sun-resistant skin.''

Raf decided she had been blessed with the most beautiful eyes he had ever seen. The most enticing body. He would do well to leave her now, before he could not. "I would still caution you to dress appropriately. I would not want you in pain. It will hinder your concentration.''

She propped her cheek on her palm. "I'll let you know if I'm hurting. That way you can be careful with me.''

"You can be assured I will always be careful with you.''

"Does the offer still stand?'' she asked.

"What offer?''

"The one about me calling you on the intercom if I need anything."

He hadn't forgotten the offer, but he'd hoped she had, otherwise he would not be able to resist her. "If you have an emergency, I will be available."

"What qualifies as an emergency?"

"I will leave that up to you."

Before he forgot his promise of patience, Raf turned away and headed to his room. He took another cool shower in an effort to reclaim his control over his body and his mind, but it was no use.

As he lay in his bed, totally nude and without any covering, he felt as though he was back in the desert surrounding his homeland of Amythra. His mouth was dry in contrast with his perspiring body. And he was as hard as he had been in a long time.

With one arm thrown over his eyes, he slid his palm down his chest, pausing below his navel, intent on relieving the deep ache Genie's presence had created as he had in the past when he'd had no choice. This time he did have a choice. He would wait until he could alleviate his need with her, and he would when the opportunity presented itself.

But his involvement with her would only entail physical pleasure. He was not open to the prospect of marriage again even though he had said as much to his younger brother, Darin—a man who had spent years traveling the world as a military tracker after suffering the loss of his fiancée, determined never to wed. Raf had made the false claim he was searching for another wife in hopes that Darin would go on with his own life. And Darin had done that two months before by marrying a woman whom he'd met on a mission as a member of the secretive Texas Cattleman's Club.

Raf remained uncertain that he would ever be willing to do the same again. However, he was not averse to finding a woman who would willingly share his bed. A woman he considered a safe haven in many ways.

Imogene Danforth could be that woman. She most likely would not add any complications or have unreasonable expectations of him. She had only one goal in mind—to be the best at her job. She would not settle for less. Nor would she be eager to settle into an ordinary life.

That suited Raf Shakir very well. He had chosen his solitary existence for valid reasons he would not reveal to her. He had no intention of changing that in the immediate future. He would also endeavor to remain patient in his pursuit of Genie Danforth.

Four

"Call me, Danforth. This is an emergency."

After listening to Sid's standard voice mail, Imogene tossed the cell phone onto the bed and fell back onto the mattress. Sid Kramer considered cold cappuccino an emergency. Most likely he couldn't find a client's file and he needed her to tell him where to locate it. She'd rather tell him where to go—someplace with a very strong furnace.

She glanced at the gold-encrusted clock on the black marble mantel. Eleven o'clock at night. Whatever had Sid's boxers in a wad couldn't be remedied at this hour. She'd call him tomorrow morning. Or wait for him to call her back. Unfortunately, that would mean keeping her cell phone on her person during her riding lesson. Somehow she got the feeling that wouldn't sit well with the sheikh. Guess she'd just have to hide the phone or put it on vibrate. She might not be able to feel it vibrate, so that was out of the question. Besides, if it did ring, she'd invite Raf to go find it, all the more reason to take it with her tomorrow.

Yes, dear Sid could wait until tomorrow, but Imogene did need to make another call that she considered important. She'd been at the stable for two days and her parents had no idea where she was or what she was doing. Normally she checked in on Sundays whenever possible, joining her family for the traditional family dinner, but yesterday she hadn't been there. She needed to let someone know where she was and why. Most likely her parents were still awake, watching the latest political coverage on Uncle Abraham's high-profile campaign.

Picking up the cell phone again, she hit the speed dial for the private number. After two rings, her mother answered with a harried, "Hello."

"Hi, Mom. It's me."

"Imogene, where are you? When you didn't come for Sunday dinner and didn't call, I was worried."

"I'm sorry. The time got away from me."

"You work…too hard."

"You sound winded, Mom. Have you and Dad been playing hide-and-seek in the wine cellar again?"

Imogene could visualize her mother giving a one-handed sweep through her blond bob while strangling the phone with the other hand. "I swear, Imogene, I thought you would have forgotten that little incident by now."

"Little incident?" Imogene teased. "You should be glad it didn't stunt my growth, seeing you and Dad making out like teenagers behind the wine racks."

Her mother cleared her throat. "For your information, young lady, your father and I have just returned from a fund-raiser for Abraham."

"Did it go well?"

"Very well. Surprisingly, the news about your cousin Marcus didn't put too much of a damper on the event."

Obviously, Imogene had fallen further out of the loop than she'd realized. "What about Marcus?"

"You haven't heard? The police called him in today to question him. They think he has something to do with the explosion at Danforth's waterfront office. They're intimating he has ties to the Colombian cartel, if you can imagine that."

Yes, she could imagine it. Too many people were bent on bringing chaos to Uncle Abraham's campaign. She wouldn't be a bit surprised if John Van Gelder, his opponent, was behind it all. "Mother, surely no one believes Marcus is involved. He's the legal counsel for Danforth & Co., for goodness' sake. The coffee business has been his life. He wouldn't risk ruining what the family has built by getting involved with criminals."

"We all know that, sweetheart. I'm praying he's cleared soon. Abraham has enough stress to deal with as it is."

By choice, Imogene thought, but didn't voice that. Abraham Danforth was basically a good man who'd made more than a few mistakes, some that were coming back to haunt him because his life had been laid bare due to his interest in politics. At least he was trying to atone, something Imogene could definitely relate to. "I'll be hoping and praying, too. Right now I need to tell you where I am so you can reach me if need be."

"You're not at work?"

"No. I'm about fifty miles northwest of Savannah, on a horse farm."

"A horse farm?" The shock resonated in her mother's tone, and not much shocked Miranda Danforth. "What on earth are you doing there?"

"Believe it or not, I'm learning to ride a horse." And learning that the man a few doors down was temptation incarnate.

"Oh, Imogene, be very careful."

"You never seemed all that concerned about my brother riding horses."

"That's different. Toby's a—"

"Man?"

"He's an expert. He knows what he's doing. I just don't want you to have an accident. I couldn't stand to lose…" Her mother's voice trailed away, but Imogene knew exactly what she'd intended to say—she couldn't stand to lose another daughter.

The same old glimmer of guilt tried to worm into Imogene's thoughts, but she pushed it away. "I'll be fine, Mom. The man who's instructing me is taking it very slowly." Too slowly.

"A man's teaching you? Is he handsome? Single?"

"Both." And more.

"What about his family? Does he have good genes?"

He looked pretty darned good in jeans, a fact Imogene did not care to discuss with her mother. "Actually, he's an Arabian sheikh."

"Royalty? That's wonderful."

Time for a subject change, before her mother went into the "it's time for you to settle down" spiel. "The place is beautiful. You'd love it, especially the furnishings. Lots of antiques. The suite I'm staying in is wonderful. Raf has been an excellent teacher, very patient and accommodating."

"Raf? You call him by his first name? Do I sense a little romance blossoming between the two of you?"

Imogene could lie and say she wasn't interested, or she could just skirt the truth. "He's not husband material, Mom, if that's what you're thinking."

"Then does he have a wine cellar?"

"Mom!" Imogene couldn't stop her laughter and neither could her mother.

After they'd sufficiently recovered, Miranda said, "It's so good to hear you laugh, Imogene. You don't do that nearly enough."

"I laugh, Mom. Maybe not all the time, but I'm not the total stuffed shirt everyone thinks I am."

"I'm sorry, sweetheart, but I just think it's high time you do something more interesting than work nonstop. I can't even remember when you've taken a break. In fact, I don't remember you taking any breaks since you turned seventeen."

Imogene had heard it all before, several times. "I know, Mom, but that goes along with my career choice."

"I understand that, but you should have some fun for a change, if you know what I mean." The last sentence was said in a conspiratorial whisper, probably so Harold Danforth wouldn't hear his wife giving their daughter permission to be a bad girl.

Imogene did not want her mother to know she was actually considering being that bad girl. "The riding is fun and fairly challenging. I'm enjoying it a lot. It's a nice break."

"You need to enjoy more than that, if the opportunity presents itself. Just be careful you don't get your heart broken again."

Little did her mother know, Imogene's heart was still intact. Wayne hadn't done that much damage, a sure sign that it hadn't been a match made in paradise. "I'll be very careful, Mom. Where's Dad?"

"In the shower, waiting for me."

That did it. Children were not supposed to know that their own parents still enjoyed shower slap and tickle. "Okay, I'm outta here before you start giving me details."

"Hugs and kisses, sweetie. I'll tell Daddy you said hello."

Imogene hung up the phone, overwhelmed by a sudden sense of longing. Her parents were fooling around, several of her cousins and her brother Jake had found love over the past few months, and she couldn't even get past the starting gate with Raf.

Sliding from the bed, Imogene walked to the double French doors and opened them wide. She stepped onto the verandah and held out the silk robe, letting the cool air flow over her heated skin while listening to the cicadas shrilling in the distance along with the mournful hoot of an owl. But the breeze and the night sounds did little to soothe her sunburn or her suddenly sullen mood. She could really use some company, but that probably wasn't going to happen, at least not tonight. It hadn't happened last night, either. If this was Raf's idea of a slow seduction, she'd be ready to leave before they got to the good part.

After going back inside, Imogene walked to the dresser and picked up the jar of homemade sunburn relief goo that Doris had given her after dinner. She unsealed the lid and took a quick sniff, expecting to detect the smell of vinegar, surprised that it smelled a little like lemons.

Heaven only knew what was in the mixture. Doris didn't strike her as the witchy type—at least not anymore—so she would just assume the cream consisted of all natural ingredients, not eye of newt or a serpent's tongue.

After discarding her robe, she scooped out a quarter's worth of the cream and rubbed it over her arms, immediately remembering Raf's hands on her during their afternoon ride the day before, something he didn't repeat today. Now wouldn't that be fun to have him rub the stuff all over her body? Wouldn't she be the foolish one to ask? Why not?

After all, her mother had told her to have some fun, and having Raf's hands on her sounded like a whole lot of fun. She certainly didn't want to disappoint Mom.

"Raf, if you're not asleep yet, I could use your help."

Raf stared at the intercom from the chair in the corner

where he'd been attempting to read the latest horse breeding magazine. He'd given up on sleep knowing that his
discomfort would continue to keep him awake for hours.
Hearing Genie's voice had only served to make the situation worse.

He walked to the intercom and depressed the button, believing it would probably be best to feign disinterest and
tell her he had, in fact, been in a deep sleep. "Yes."

"Oh. You *are* up."

"I most definitely am now. What do you need?"

"It's my sunburn. I know you said I shouldn't contact
you unless it's an emergency, but I'm having trouble reach-
ing my back to apply the lotion. Could you help me out?"

Helping her out of her clothing immediately came to
mind. But he supposed he could maintain his resolve for a
short while in order to relieve her discomfort. In turn, he
would probably only add to his own. "I will be there in a
moment."

Raf didn't bother wearing a robe. After all, she had seen
him shirtless twice before. Unfortunately, he had only seen
her fully clothed, yet that had not mattered in terms of his
attraction to her. He hoped she remained clothed tonight,
otherwise he was in grave danger of disregarding patience
for the prospect of pleasure.

He rapped twice on her door and only seconds passed
before she answered. She did happen to be dressed, although Raf would not deem the clothing as modest. The
short ivory silk robe gaped open, revealing a scrap of a
matching silk gown that came to the tops of her thighs. The
neckline scooped low, barely concealing the rise of her
breasts but not the shading of her nipples that showed beneath the fabric. Yet he noticed immediately that her skin
was reddened, much more so than it had been at dinner.
And so was her nose, not that she had lost any of her

appeal. But his resistance would be in peril if he did not remain detached.

"Come in," she said and opened the door wide, allowing him entry. "I really appreciate this. I didn't realize how much sun I'd gotten or that the shirt left so much of my back exposed."

She moved with grace to the dressing table, the robe flowing behind her. After retrieving a jar of white lotion, she turned and presented it to him. "Doris claims this will help. If you'll just put a little of this on my upper back and neck, I should be good as new until morning."

Raf was as good as lost when she turned and shimmied the robe down her arms where it drifted to the floor in a pool of satin. He could see in great detail the curve of her buttocks, enough to drive him near madness.

She faced him again and said, "Where do you want me?"

"I am not certain I understand the question."

"Do you want me to stand?" She pointed at the black woven rug on the floor at the side of the bed facing the hearth. "How about I sit there?"

Regardless of where she sat, he could not ignore her or the fire building in his groin. At least she had not suggested the bed. "The chaise would be adequate. Or perhaps the vanity stool."

"Oh, come on. The carpet's wonderful. I've wanted to see if it's as soft as it looks since the first time I laid eyes on it."

Raf was wondering the same about her. "I suppose the rug will do, if that is what you wish."

Genie took her place on the floor, legs stretched before her as she faced the mirrored wall. He perched on the edge of the mattress behind her and took the lotion she offered over one shoulder, hollowing out a handful of the cream before setting the jar beside her on the floor. She tipped her head forward, giving him access to her slender neck and shoulders that had suffered the most exposure due to the shorter cut of her hair.

Raf hesitated for a long moment, knowing that if he touched her—when he touched her—his control would begin to slip. And so did the straps of Genie's nightgown when she lifted her shoulders.

"Something wrong, Raf?" Her voice was quiet, almost teasing, as if she knew exactly what she was doing to him. Most likely she did.

"My hands are callused," he said. "I do not wish to hurt you."

"I know you'll be gentle."

If she only knew how badly he wanted to tear away her gown and pull her into the bed, then she might question his gentleness. Yet he took extra care as he rubbed the cream over her shoulders, finding her soft skin against his palms most pleasurable. He had greatly missed the texture of a woman's flesh, the scent of her hair, the frailness of her frame in contrast with his. Memories of another woman assailed him. Bitter recollections of a relationship that had begun with anger, then ended in disaster.

Raf pushed those thoughts aside and concentrated on these moments with a woman he wanted more than anything he could recall in the recent past.

Genie stared at him through the reflection, her green eyes sparkling. "I think you can get to me better if you'll come down on my level."

She was most definitely getting to him. All of him, and the muslin material of his pajamas could do nothing to hide that evidence unless he did join her on the floor. But then she would most likely feel the effect she was having on him. Perhaps that was not such a bad idea. Tonight, he would only begin to demonstrate his passion for her, carefully. Slowly.

Raf slid onto the floor, extended his legs alongside her legs and gathered more of the lotion into his palm. Bringing his arms around her, he applied the balm to the center of her chest beneath her slender throat, working his way down but only in small increments.

From the mirror's reflection, he met Imogene's gaze and he saw desire in her languid eyes. Her lips parted, her chest rose with each breath she took, faster with every pass he made over the rise of her breasts. Her respiration seemed to stop altogether when he rested his lips against her neck, their gazes still connected in anticipation.

"You are very beautiful," he told her as he palmed her breasts lightly through the satin.

She murmured, "Thank you," but he saw hesitancy in her eyes. That hesitancy gave him pause. As stalwart as she had been since they'd met, the vulnerability in her expression endeared her to him in many ways. He understood all too well why she had hidden this side from him, for at times he had learned that was preferable. However, he did not know why she seemed insecure or who had been responsible. He only knew that he wanted to show her how much he appreciated her simple beauty. He wanted her to experience what he was feeling at the moment.

Slowly, his mind cautioned his body. Savor her. Savor this.

When Genie leaned her head back against his chest, he tilted her chin toward him and drew her into a kiss, exploring her warm mouth with his tongue while he continued to fondle her breasts through the gown.

He could taste her need mingled with his own, sensed it in the way she circled his neck with one hand, pulling him closer, deeper into the heat of her mouth. In that instance, he craved being inside her as much as he'd craved his solitude.

He broke the kiss to whisper, "Watch," again drawing

her gaze to the reflection. Slowly he lowered the gown to bare her breasts to his eyes and hands. As he'd predicted, her nipples were a soft shade of coral and he wanted to know how they would feel in his mouth, against his tongue. Instead he gently rolled them between his fingertips while squeezing her thighs together with his thighs, knowing that if he touched her at the apex, he would find her hot and damp. But he would not do that tonight. He intended this to be only the prelude. By the time they made love, she would be totally on the edge, as would he. Then he would uncover the sensual facets of her being and have her willingly take all that he had to give, at least physically. All that he had held back for two years.

In order to do that, he would have to leave her soon. Yet, at the moment, she looked so beautiful that he could not stand the thought of leaving her. But he must. If he did not, he most likely would remove her gown and make love to her in spite of his promise to proceed with caution and care.

"I must go," he said as he came to his feet.

Genie pulled the gown back into place and stood, her expression presenting confusion and the remnants of desire. "Where are you going?"

"To bed. You should do the same. Otherwise you will be too tired for your lesson."

Anger turned her eyes to fire. "You know something, Raf Shakir, you are nothing but a big tease."

"I've told you we will take this slowly."

"And I still have no say in the matter?"

He reached out and cupped her jaw. "Do you not find the anticipation exciting? Do you not see that by waiting, when we finally do make love, it will be all that you've ever desired and more?"

"You are so damned sure of yourself, aren't you?"

"Are you not sure of yourself?"

Her gaze faltered. "Most of the time."

Lifting her chin, he forced her to look at him once more. "I have no doubt that you will be as proficient a lover as you are a businesswoman."

"Thanks for the vote of confidence. I hope neither of us will be disappointed."

He leaned over and brushed a kiss across her lips. "That will never happen."

Her expression brightened. "You're right, I don't think I'll be disappointed at all, if you know what to do with this."

Taking Raf by surprise, Genie ran a fingertip down the middle of his chest, down his abdomen and onto his erection that lurched beneath her touch.

Before he changed his mind and hastened his plan, he pulled her hand away, kissed her palm and walked out the door. He would probably need more than a night to restore his control, and to analyze why he suddenly felt as if his life was about to change. Change was not always good even if at times inevitable. The last change he'd endured had nearly destroyed him.

Logic told him to hold tightly to his emotions when he held Genie. Yet his grip seemed to be tenuous. He did not want to feel anything for her beyond fondness because she would eventually leave him, and he would not stop her no matter how much he cared for her.

Imogene generally dealt in logic, but this overwhelming need for Raf Shakir wasn't logical at all. Nor was his mood this afternoon after what had transpired between them last night. The same surly mood he'd displayed that morning during her lessons. He stood in the middle of the arena like a circus ringmaster, gratefully minus the whip. She rode on the dinky English saddle atop Maurice, her jaw clenched like a vise to keep the retorts at bay while he dealt out orders like a drill sergeant. More knee pressure! Straighten your frame! Grip the reins loosely! Make him answer your cues! Go to hell on a post-hole digger, was the one Imogene really wanted to hurl back.

Today it seemed she could do absolutely nothing right in his eyes. But last night…

She wondered if his sour disposition had anything to do with last night. Maybe he regretted what he'd done. Maybe he'd begun to reconsider. Maybe he'd sensed her insecurity about her own abilities in the lovemaking department. She most definitely wasn't a virgin, but her experience had been limited to Wayne. Wayne had been a considerate lover, if not that inspired. Those experiences would probably pale in comparison to what Raf intended for her. If he intended anything other than grilling her on her lousy horsemanship.

As she walked the pen under his scrutiny, even when he looked as if he could spit fire, Imogene couldn't stop thinking about their interlude. Having him touch her in front of the mirror had been the most erotic experience of her life. And although it would be categorized as only minor petting, she had never, ever been so attuned to her sensuality. Nor had she ever wanted to make love so urgently. On the up side, he had promised her it would eventually happen between them, if he hadn't changed his mind. The suspense might literally kill her, if he didn't first.

When her cell phone began to ring, Raf looked much more furious than frustrated. She tugged Maurice to a stop, reached beneath her shirt and withdrew the phone from the holder hooked to her waistband.

"Danforth, why the hell didn't you call me back?"

"I'm in the middle of a riding lesson, Sid. I'll call you back later."

"This can't wait. I have to know when—"

Imogene never heard the last of Sid's request because Raf yanked the phone from her grasp, told Sid in a stern voice,

"Ms. Danforth is not to be disturbed," then snapped off the phone.

Imogene finally closed her mouth. "Why did you do that?"

"Are you serious about learning?" he asked, his eyes narrowed into a harsh glare.

"That happened to be my boss. He wouldn't have called unless it was important." And that was the biggest tall tale she had ever told.

"Again I ask, are you serious about learning."

"I'm here, aren't I? I'm here and I'm enduring your irritable behavior and your commands and I haven't issued one complaint. Yet."

"If what you say is true, then you will not bring this again." He held up the phone. "Not if you want to be safe. You are fortunate the horse did not balk."

Imogene looked down at Maurice with his snout practically resting in the dirt. Most likely, he was soundly sleeping. She patted his neck and he still didn't stir. Good God, did horses croak while standing up? Thankfully his ear twitched, proving he had not moved on to the horsey hereafter. "I can tell the phone really upset Maurice and roused him from his coma."

Raf didn't seem to appreciate her sarcasm, evidenced by his scowl. "I have witnessed riders severely injured due to less distraction. You are still a novice."

The severity of his tone made Imogene internally flinch. It also made her curious. "Someone you knew well?"

"That does not matter."

Oh, but it did matter to Imogene. From the troubled look in his eyes, she suspected this was personal experience talking. She saluted in hopes of lightening his mood. "Yes, Your Highness. Is there anything else you would like to chastise me about?"

His demeanor was anything but light. "I told you to wear long sleeves, did I not?"

She glanced at her bare arms. "Yes, but my skin is fine. The burn's already faded." Sort of, Imogene decided when she noted a deeper tinge of pink. So much for the ten reapplications of sunblock.

"You are going to be in pain again tonight."

She sent him a sunny smile. "That's why I have Doris's trusty sunburn solution. Maybe you could help me out again."

"The lesson is over," he said, and left the pen.

Imogene's heart sank to her boots when she realized he was regretting last night, and he probably had no intention of following through with his promise of lovemaking. She definitely had something to say about that.

After climbing clumsily off Maurice, she tugged him behind her and into the barn where she found Raf mucking out the stall. He'd removed his shirt, affording Imogene a first-rate view of his jean-covered butt and bare back.

She toed the sawdust with her boot and sneezed three times, figuring that would get his attention. When he didn't acknowledge her, she asked, "What do you want me to do with Maurice?"

He continued to shovel the shavings, discarding the debris in the wheelbarrow with a vengeance. "Remove his bridle and put the halter on him. Then brush his coat. Blaylock will rinse him before he is put up for the night."

That she could do. Maurice, cooperative as ever, just stood there while Imogene fumbled with the bridle and replaced it with the halter. Too bad his owner wasn't as compliant today. He would be, if she had any say-so in the matter, and she definitely would.

After she had Maurice's coat displaying a nice sheen, Imogene tossed the brush into the grooming cart next to the stall and stood in the open doorway. "Could I have my phone back please?"

He leaned the shovel against the wall, then finally faced her. "Why do you need it now?"

Stubborn man. "Because it's mine."

He raked her body with a long visual excursion, then hooked his thumbs in his belt loops. Imogene's gaze zipped to his front pocket where she saw the outline of her phone. At least she thought it was her phone. "You know, you could've put it on vibrate mode and had loads of fun if Sid called back, which he probably did. I'm sure he's royally ticked off at us both."

"Your boss is not my concern."

"That's easy for you to say. You don't work for him." She held out her open palm. "Now let me have it."

"Come get it."

A thick silence hung over the barn as they stared at each other like gunslingers confronting each other at high noon. Challenge called out from Raf's magnetic gray eyes, pulling Imogene forward to stand face-to-face with a solid, sweating male.

She brushed her knuckles down his chest, reached for the phone in his pocket and withdrew it slowly. His jaw went taut and so did the six-pack of muscles in his belly. Then in a rush, he clasped her waist and backed her against the stall, bracing one hand next to her head but keeping his lower body angled away from her. "Do not wear that shirt again."

"Would you prefer I rode topless?" She traced a path around his nipple with a finger. "Oh, but I guess you're concerned with my sun exposure, so that probably wouldn't do."

"I am concerned with my ability to concentrate on your lesson. I cannot do that when you distract me."

"How do I distract you?"

"With your body." He emphasized his words by cupping her breast in one large palm. "With your mouth. Your eyes."

"Are you suggesting I wear a trench coat, a blindfold and a gag?"

"A regular blouse would suffice."

Awareness finally dawned, and it made Imogene want to shout with victory. "Is that what had you in such a bad mood today? Was I distracting you?"

He took her hand and held it against his erection. "What do you think?"

She thought she was about to faint dead away, or melt onto the sawdust floor like a tub of butter. "That's not all my fault. You could've done something about this..." She pressed her palm against him. "Last night."

"Last night would not have been the best time."

She challenged him with a look, with a smooth stroke of her hand. "Then do something about it now."

Imogene's fantasy from the first time they'd met—passion in the barn with a stranger, even though Raf was no longer a stranger. Yet she still didn't know what lurked behind the secrecy in his eyes or the troubles binding his heart. She did recognize that her previous imaginings could not do justice to Raf's sudden kiss. A kiss more spicy than sweet, more desperate than delicate. More than she could have hoped for.

Masculine shouts in the distance, the occasional whinny, could not stop what was happening between them. Even Imogene's cautious side went the way of the breeze blowing into the barn and stirring up dust. The kiss, so deliciously hot and decadent, was beginning to stir up trouble. She couldn't deny that her body was giving her plenty of signals that if Raf commanded she remove her clothes and take what he had to offer right there, right now, she would gladly do it. She had no choice. Nature, not good sense, called to her now, even when Raf snaked his hand beneath her shirt and bra. This was no meeting of the minds. This was pure electricity, the preparation for pleasure.

Raf showed no signs of stopping when he weighed her bare breast in his palm. He did show her signs of how he had been affected by this frenzied bout of foreplay by pressing harder against her. He continued his sultry assault on her mouth, using his tongue in the most wild and wicked ways to convey a message that wasn't totally lost on Imogene.

Without giving her the opportunity to draw a breath, or to reconcile all the reasons why they really should stop, he skimmed one hand down her belly and yanked the hook at her waistband, then slowly slid down the zipper of her riding pants. She heard the rasp of his own fly and realized that in about ten seconds, it would be too late to stop this insanity. Better crazy and satisfied than sensible and unfulfilled, was Imogene's last thought before Raf worked his hand inside her breeches.

"Do you want me to work the mare, Sheikh Shakir?" someone shouted.

Imogene just wanted him to go away. Instead, Raf went away, taking all his magic when he pushed back from her.

Imogene blinked twice as if that might restore her sense of reality. Raf had turned his back to her, his hands laced behind his neck as he stared up at the ceiling. "Yes," he called back to the unknown intruder while Imogene regrouped and readjusted her clothes.

Raf wasn't as hasty in his refastening but finally did bring his hands from his nape to his fly. The sound of his rising zipper wasn't nearly as exciting to Imogene as it had been being lowered.

She touched her fingertips to her lips, finding them tender and sensitive. Still, she would gladly endure more of that sweet, sweet torture for one more of Raf's kisses. But right now, he wouldn't even look at her.

"I'll head back to the house now," she said. Back to analyze what had just happened and to pout over the interruption.

"I believe that would be best."

She walked past him and he still didn't bother to face her. "Guess I'll see you later."

"Perhaps at dinner."

At least it was something. Imogene trudged back up the path with an oddly heavy heart, burdened by the fact that somehow this whole arrangement no longer had to do with business.

She was growing far too fond of the stoic sheikh, and it wasn't just about the prospect of great sex, although she couldn't deny she wanted him. She admittedly wanted to know more about him, even if that meant crossing the boundaries between a little physical fun and emotional involvement.

But something wasn't quite right with him. Something had him warring with their mutual attraction. She'd never been all that good at reading men, so she could be totally off base. But maybe, just maybe, she might find out a little more the next time they were alone. If they were ever alone again.

Five

___

Raf needed to be alone. He needed to find a place where he could reclaim his control. Bracing his hands on the wall, he lowered his head and closed his eyes. He could still taste Genie, could still smell her rose perfume on his body. He could still see her face and the need, the passion building between them. He had wanted to see that so badly, he had forgotten his promise to take it slowly. Had they not been interrupted, he would have taken her instead.

"She is ready now."

Raf looked to the aisle to see Ali Kahmir standing in the doorway, the only worker who had been willing to accompany him to America. The rest had chosen to stay behind in Amythra due to Raf's inability to control his overwhelming anger following the tragic accident that had changed his life. After he had effectively driven his people away, he had vowed to keep his temper in check and had done so until this morning with Genie. She did not deserve the brunt of his frustration nor would she understand the root of his torment. Only he knew his own remorse and the cause. He would keep it that way. In order to do that, he must take time to restore order to his emotions.

Pushing away from the wall, Raf strode through the door and down the aisle.

"Are you certain you wish to do this?" Ali asked from behind him.

Raf did not bother to face his long-time friend. He could not bear to see the pity in the man's expression. "It is long past time I do this."

"Why today?"

Raf had asked himself that same thing this morning when he'd made the decision. Perhaps he needed a solid reminder of why he needed to treat Genie with great care. "Today is as good as any. Did you put her through the groundwork as I requested?"

"Yes. She still has some difficulty with her right lead. Otherwise, she has appeared to have mastered the rest."

"Good. I will take it from here."

When Raf approached the arena where the chestnut mare was tied, he immediately noticed she had grown in the past two years, now well above sixteen hands. She had been his special project, half Arabian, half Hanoverian, bred for height and strength in order to bring interest in Olympic-level dressage to his stables in Amythra. She had been his hope, and in part, responsible for his slide into despair. But he could not blame the mare; he was to blame.

Raf spoke to her softly as he untied the reins and led her outside the arena. When he mounted the saddle, she stood submissively, very different from the last time he had attempted to ride her two years before, thanks to Ali's mastery. He started down the path leading to the river, content to allow the mare to walk at an easy gait. After a time, he cued her into a trot. She seemed satisfied with that for a while but he could sense she wanted to run. So did Raf.

With little effort, he cued her into a canter then into a gallop, faster and faster, her flaxen mane flowing in the wind. Even when he reached the point where the path narrowed and open fields gave way to heavy foliage, he let her run. He ducked to miss the thick overhang, leaning low at her neck. He wanted to close his eyes to banish the images—a dangerous prospect in light of the terrain. Yet he acknowledged that no matter how far or how fast he ran, the memories would still come, keen as a knife's blade. They always had.

At the water's edge, Raf pulled the mare to a stop and dismounted, winded and weary when he should have been exhilarated over the ride. He dropped the reins and let the mare graze on what little grass had managed to grow beneath the thick cypress overhang. He leaned back against the trunk of one gnarled tree, only mildly aware of the sounds of wildlife echoing from the swampy terrain, and tried to recapture his respiration, his sense of calm. It was no use.

With the mare nearby, he could only recall the events, turning them over in his mind, questioning once more what he could have done differently to change the outcome of that horrific April day two years before.

He should never have married Daliya. He had been thirty-four at the time; she had been only twenty and too young to assume the role of wife to a prince. Yet Raf had let duty dictate his life partner. Duty to produce an heir. Duty to adhere to the terms of marrying a woman he'd been ordained to wed as it had been for generations. As it had been for his own mother and father.

He had also rushed Daliya into his bed. Granted, she had gone willingly, as she'd been expected to do, but he'd witnessed no passion in her eyes, no desire for him—only defiance. No matter what he had done to accommodate her, she had not responded favorably to his efforts. Nor had she responded to his touch, or at least she had not wanted to. She seemed to resent him when he'd brought her pleasure and he'd made certain he had before he had seen to his own. During the few times they had made love, his body had been sated, but his soul had been empty.

Two weeks following their wedding, he had given her the mare in an attempt to make her somewhat happy. He'd also given her instructions not to ride the green-broke horse until he had worked with them both longer. Daliya had gone against his wishes and made a grave error by setting off across the palace grounds at a gallop. She had also attempted to jump a low wall and in doing so, fell to her death while Raf had helplessly looked on.

If only he had tried harder to stop her. If only he had been able to make her happy. Instead, he had refused to listen to her arguments, she had run away and in doing so, met her demise.

The memories came back as if the accident had happened only moments before. He had hurried to Daliya's side to hold her and only then had he realized he could have been more patient with her. He could have grown to love her even if she had never been able to love him. He should have given her the freedom she had craved, her request that fateful morning. That had been his shame. That had been the only time—the last time—that he had cried in his adulthood. And that had been the moment he'd vowed never to marry again.

As the wind picked up in intensity and storm clouds gathered overhead, Raf retrieved the mare and decided to go by foot back to the stables. She seemed satisfied to follow along quietly, unaware that she had been the catalyst for the resurrection of Raf's remorse, and his failed attempts to bring peace to his marriage. He had even renamed her Daliya so he would never forget his downfall. And he had come to America to begin a new life, severing all ties to his homeland now that his father was dead, and hoping to erase the memories, to no avail.

Raf supposed in many ways he had chosen this day to bring the memories out as a reminder of what he could not allow to happen with Genie. He wanted her desperately yet he would not make love to her unless he was certain that was what she wanted, as well. He would continue to take his time and make sure she knew her own mind. Never again would he take a woman to his bed if she was not there by her own choice, if she did not want his attentions.

He had ways to find out if Genie truly wanted him, and he would practice them tonight. Perhaps he would find the solace he craved in her arms, even if that solace was short-lived. Even if peace would always elude him.

From her bedroom window, Imogene watched Raf return to the house, his dark hair reflecting the last rays of the setting sun. The remnants of a tropical depression had passed them by without releasing more than a minimal shower. But the storm in Raf's expression was very apparent, even at this distance.

As he drew closer, Imogene realized she had never seen such sadness in a man's eyes. She *had* seen that same sadness in her own eyes when she'd looked into the mirror only a few moments ago. In part she was sad that he hadn't joined her for dinner. In part because she'd just awakened abruptly from a dream involving her sister—sweet, trusting Tori, standing in a field, arms outstretched, her amber blond hair blowing away from her face to reveal eyes a near match in color to her long, straight locks. Since Tori's disappearance from the concert five years before, Imogene had dreamed of her often, always the same dream—running toward her on leaden feet, waving like mad and calling her name, only to have Tori dissolve before she could reach her.

Imogene didn't understand why Tori had appeared in the middle of the pasture at SaHráa Stables instead of back home in their own backyard, the dream's usual setting. But she didn't have the energy to analyze the vision. Right now she only wanted to take a hot soak in the tub, take the thriller novel she'd brought with her onto the verandah and try to solve the mystery. She certainly couldn't begin to solve the mystery of the dream or of Raf Shakir. She seriously doubted he would ever divulge that much of himself to her. She was beginning to wonder if he would ever show up again, at least outside the confines of the riding pen.

Imogene managed to get her bath, but before she could even pick up the book, her cell phone rang.

"Why the hell did you hang up on me, Danforth?"

Ah, dear Sid. He had such warmth. "I told you I was in the middle of a riding lesson, didn't I?"

"Bad form, Danforth. It's chaos around here. I can't find the Littleton file."

"Did you try looking under *L?*"

"I'm not dumb, Danforth."

That was highly debatable. "Did you check with the admin?"

"No. What's her name?"

Oh, brother. "Rachel. She's been there seven years. I think you should introduce yourself."

"I don't have time to make nicey-nice with a secretary. If you were here, I wouldn't be having those problems."

If she were there, he might find himself on the wrong end of a letter opener. "Calm down, Sid."

"I can't calm down. The market's nuts right now."

"Sorry, Sid, but I don't have any control over that. How are you going to settle nervous investors if you sound like you're ready for a padded cell?"

"That's your job, Danforth, so you better hurry up with this horse thing and get back here immediately."

"I'm not ready yet." Not ready to make a good showing for the Granthams. Not ready to leave Raf.

"I'll give you until the middle of next week."

"Two full weeks, otherwise I'm wasting my time."

"End of next week, and that's my final offer."

"I'll see what I can do to accelerate my expertise." And hopefully accelerate Raf into making good on his promise. She didn't want to leave before she knew what it would be like to have him in her bed.

"I'm going to bed soon, Sid. Is there anything else?"

"Enjoy yourself."

She definitely planned to do that, if she ever got Raf alone again. "Okay, Sid. Have a drink." Or two or three.

Without bothering with goodbye, Sid hung up and Imogene walked onto the verandah. She settled on the comfy chaise with the book, but all she could think of was Raf and how he'd held her that afternoon. How he had dispelled any doubts about where she wanted this thing between them to go. But considering his absence, it might not go anywhere.

The sexual tug-of-war might be driving her crazy, but not enough for her to make the next move this time. If he wanted to see this through, he would simply have to come to her.

When she heard the rap on the door an hour later, Imogene inclined her head to make certain she'd heard correctly. It came again, loud enough to drown out the pulse thrumming in her ears. She rushed to the door on the wings of anticipation, only to find Doris on the other side dressed in a hot-pink and lime-green floral housecoat, her hair tucked beneath a pink satin turban.

"Hi, sugar. Just wondering if you need any clean sheets."

She needed a lover, not linens. She needed Raf. "Nope. I'm fine."

Doris looked somewhat satisfied but she didn't look at all as though she wanted to leave. In fact, she scanned the room as if searching for something, or someone. "Well, okay, if you don't need anything, I'll be going on to bed now."

"Sweet dreams, Doris."

"You, too, sugar. Hope you get plenty of sleep. And if you don't, I hope it's because you have something more important to occupy your time."

Doris snickered as she strolled down the hallway, taking her sweet time.

Expelling a groan, Imogene started back to the verandah only to be stopped again by a knock. Obviously Doris wanted to chat and Imogene frankly was not up to the company.

She threw open the door but this time Doris wasn't darkening her threshold. Raf was, all six feet, four inches of top-grade male dressed in a pair of black pajama bottoms covered by a plain white T-shirt. His hair was damp, his lips outlined by a spattering of evening whiskers. He smelled like a summer shower, and he looked like admission to ecstasy.

"May I come in?"

Like he really had to ask. Imogene stepped aside and allowed him entry, took a deep breath then closed the door and faced him. "I was beginning to wonder if you planned to spend the night in the stable."

"Not presently, but that could be necessary in the future. I have a mare who's expecting BáHar's first offspring. We had some trouble getting her in foal so she is the last to deliver."

Imogene's business side kicked in despite Raf's very welcome arrival. "Is that her fault or BáHar's?"

"She is an older mare, so it is not uncommon."

"Good. I wouldn't want prospective investors in the syndication believing BáHar can't get the job done."

"I assure you he can."

Like horse, like owner, Imogene thought, then felt heat immediately blanket her face. "BáHar and the mare had no trouble getting together?"

"We had no problem collecting from him."

"Collecting?"

"Semen. The procedure is done artificially."

Imogene wasn't sure how that was accomplished, or if she even wanted to know. "That can't be too much fun for BáHar."

"He hasn't seemed to mind the breeding dummy as long as we have a teasing mare present. You should watch the process some time."

Dummy? Teasing mare? "No, thanks. That would make me feel like a voyeur."

"It is all very clinical and controlled. BáHar would be none the wiser if you observed."

Imogene would be extremely embarrassed. "I think I'll just take your word for it."

"That is your option, but you might wish to learn the workings of the business in order for you to advise me on the syndication."

"I can deal with the numbers and you can deal with the mating rituals."

His eyes took on that nighttime intensity. "Perhaps we should discuss mating rituals further."

Imogene didn't really want to talk about it, she just wanted to do it. And heavens, they almost had in the barn.

Without an invitation, Raf moved to the bed and took a seat. Imogene joined him, keeping her distance until she knew why he had come. She hoped he was here for more of the same of what they'd shared last night. To finish what they'd begun that morning. Maybe if it finally happened, she could go about the business of learning to ride and get this all out of her system. And that was about as likely as Sid finding the file without blow-by-blow instructions.

He scooted to the edge of the mattress and folded his hands together, elbows resting on his thighs. "First, I would like to apologize."

Imogene's hopes shattered. "Apologize for what?"

"For the way I treated you earlier today."

This was not at all what she wanted to hear. "It just happened, Raf. We got a little carried away."

"I do not apologize for that, although I am sorry I lost control. I meant the anger I displayed. It was directed at you, but not about you."

Imogene's curiosity climbed. "Then what was it about?"

"That does not matter. I only want you to know it has nothing to do with you."

"Are you sure? Maybe I'm not progressing fast enough in the riding department." She hated the insecurity in her voice.

Raf gave her a reassuring smile. "As I've told you, you're doing well for the short time you've been here."

"Thanks."

He sent a long glance down her body. "Red suits you."

Imogene cinched the sash tighter. "Are you referring to my skin or my nightgown?"

"Your nightgown, although I have no complaints about your skin."

She figured her face was a perfect match to the short satin negligee, both from the heat in his gaze and the fact she'd never been good at accepting compliments graciously. She wanted to say, "Why, this old thing?" but in reality, she'd worn it for him. Worn it because she'd hoped he would come back to her tonight. Here he was, and she had no idea what to say, what to do. Very odd, considering she'd always been able to think on her feet during business dealings. But again, this fantastic, forbidden attraction to him had nothing to do with business.

"Thanks again." That sounded so lame, but she didn't have enough presence of mind to come up with something more original, especially when he continued to stare at her as if waiting for her to do something. Waiting for her to make some kind of move.

Imogene knew what she wanted to do, but she couldn't muster enough courage to ask. Instead, "I guess you're probably ready for bed," came out of her runaway mouth. "I mean, I'm sure you're tired."

"Are you tired?" he asked in that deep, persuasive tone that encouraged tingles to play up and down her spine.

"Not really."

"Is your sunburn bothering you?"

She swept a hand through her hair, realizing she had barely run a comb through it since leaving her bath. "Actually, it's still a little tender."

"Would you like me to assist you again? It's the least I can do considering my disregard for your feelings."

"You didn't hurt my feelings exactly."

"I would still like to make it up to you."

"I wouldn't object to your attention."

The tension between them was almost palpable and the silence stretched between them. Then he rose with masculine grace and took her hand to pull her from the bed. He left only long enough to retrieve the lotion and set the jar down on the small end table. Then he turned his beautiful eyes to Imogene and untied her sash slowly, sliding his hands beneath the fabric at her shoulders and working it off her arms. He again paused to take a visual excursion down her body, lingering at her breasts. Her nipples turned to tight knots under his perusal and her stomach fluttered along with her heart.

She almost groaned when he headed away from her as if he'd reconsidered. She released a breath of relief when she realized he was only dimming the lights to a soft glow, setting the mood, she supposed, although she didn't need anything to put her in the mood. He'd done that when he'd shown up in her suite.

The open verandah doors allowed a jasmine-scented draft to seep into the room and provided a breathtaking backdrop of stars. When he came back to her, he didn't ask her where she wanted to be, what she wanted him to do. He knew, just as he knew how to hold her prisoner with only a look.

Raf brought her down to the floor facing the mirrored wall again, much the same as they had last night, his legs wrapped around her legs like a sensual cocoon. He dipped his hand into the open jar and nudged her forward to apply the lotion to her upper back where her hair didn't cover her exposed skin. His callused hands became velvet as he soothed his palms over her shoulders and down her arms, moving across her chest where the half moon shape of red-dened skin ended at the top of her breasts. But this time, he didn't touch her beyond that. He did rest his palms on her shoulders and his lips against her ear. "Anything else you wish me to do, you will have to show me."

She was grateful he hadn't said she had to tell him what she wanted because frankly, she wasn't sure she could speak. But she could show him, and she began by pulling her arms from the straps and lowering her gown. When he failed to move his palms from her shoulders, she reached up and brought his hands to her breasts. As he'd done the night before, he finessed them with his skilled fingertips until Imogene craved more than only his touch.

After shifting slightly, she draped her arm around his neck and nudged his head down where he feathered warm, wet kisses over her throat before sliding his tongue between the cleft of her breasts. She showed him exactly what she

An Important Message from the Editors

Dear Reader,

Because you've chosen to read one of our fine romance novels, we'd like to say "thank you!" And, as a special way to thank you, we've selected two more of the books you love so well, plus an exciting Mystery Gift, to send you absolutely FREE!

Please enjoy them with our compliments...

Pam Powers

Peel off Seal and Place Inside...

How to validate your Editor's
FREE GIFT
"Thank You"

1. Peel off gift seal from front cover. Place it in space provided at right. This automatically entitles you to receive 2 FREE BOOKS and a fabulous mystery gift.

2. Send back this card and you'll get 2 brand-new Silhouette Desire® novels. These books have a cover price of $4.25 each in the U.S. and $4.99 each in Canada, but they are yours to keep absolutely free.

3. There's no catch. You're under no obligation to buy anything. We charge nothing—ZERO—for your first shipment. And you don't have to make any minimum number of purchases—not even one!

4. The fact is, thousands of readers enjoy receiving their books by mail from the Silhouette Reader Service™. They enjoy the convenience of home delivery...they like getting the best new novels at discount prices BEFORE they're available in stores...and they love their *Heart to Heart* subscriber newsletter featuring author news, horoscopes, recipes, book reviews and much more!

5. We hope that after receiving your free books you'll want to remain a subscriber. But the choice is yours— to continue or cancel, any time at all! So why not take us up on our invitation, with no risk of any kind. You'll be glad you did!

6. Remember...just for validating your Editor's Free Gift Offer, we'll send you THREE gifts, *ABSOLUTELY FREE!*

GET A *Free* MYSTERY GIFT...

*SURPRISE MYSTERY GIFT COULD BE YOURS **FREE** AS A SPECIAL "THANK YOU" FROM THE EDITORS OF SILHOUETTE*

The Editor's "Thank You" Free Gifts Include:

- Two BRAND-NEW romance novels!
- An exciting mystery gift!

Yes I have placed my Editor's "Thank You" seal in the space provided above. Please send me 2 free books and a fabulous Mystery Gift. I understand I am under no obligation to purchase any books, as explained on the back and on the opposite page.

326 SDL DZ6P   **225 SDL DZ64**

FIRST NAME	LAST NAME

ADDRESS

APT.#	CITY

STATE/PROV.	ZIP/POSTAL CODE

(S-D-06/04)

Thank You!

▲ DETACH AND MAIL CARD TODAY! ▼

wanted and where she wanted it by guiding his head down
until his warm lips encompassed her nipple.

A sigh slipped out as she combed her fingers through his
thick hair and held on as if he were a lifeline. In many
ways he was, since he had effortlessly brought her back to
the land of the living. Every pass of his tongue, every pull
of his mouth, made her feel as alive as she'd ever been. As
needy as she'd ever been.

When she made a faint sound of pleasure, he lifted his
head and sought her eyes. "Do you require something else
of me tonight?"

"Yes."

"Then show me."

After planting a soft kiss on each breast, then one on her
mouth, he pulled her arm away and turned her back toward
the mirror. Imogene recognized he knew what she wanted,
what she needed, but still he waited until she made the next
move. And she did by clasping the hem of her gown and
pulling it over her head, leaving her completely exposed
except for the pair of matching red panties. His arms came
around her, his warm brown skin standing out against the
fair flesh on her belly. In the mirror's reflection, she mar-
veled at the size of his hands and how he used them so
gently when he slid one down to her navel and with the
other cupped her breast, playing his thumb back and forth
over her nipple.

All the inhibitions Imogene had possessed until that moment came tumbling down as she nudged Raf's hand lower.
She held her breath, waiting, watching for the moment he
took the lead. He didn't disappoint her when he whispered,
"Open for me," as he urged her legs apart with his palm
on the inside of her thighs. She wasn't quite brave enough
to remove her panties and he seemed to sense that when
he didn't try to slide them down. He did slide his hand
beneath the lace band. That alone caused Imogene's legs

to tremble and sent a rush of dampness between her thighs. In some ways, she felt as if she had left her body, watching the scene play out in the mirror. In other ways, she had never been so in tune with her body, her own sensuality that had lain dormant for so long.

Even though she couldn't see what he was doing, she could feel it. Oh, could she feel it—the silken stroke of his fingers over her, inside her, the sensation of fullness, building pressure with every caress. He plied her neck with kisses, held her close, fondled her breasts, kept the torrent of feelings coming and coming until Imogene couldn't hold on anymore.

The climax hit her in a hard succession of swells until she slowly drifted back into reality, only to be thrust back into a world of sensation when Raf palmed her cheek and brought his lips to hers for a kiss that was the perfect culmination of the experience. Yet he didn't stop touching her, caressing her, cajoling her with his steady strokes until he urged another climax from her.

She ducked her head beneath his chin and let go a long, steady moan that would have turned into a scream had she not bitten her lip to stop it.

As fiercely determined as Raf had seemed to be to show her this pleasure, he was also determined to show her a sensitive side when he pulled her into his lap, into his arms, her face resting against his heart that beat so steadily against her cheek. A heart that she wanted to know, inside out. More important, she wanted to know how it would be to have him inside her, completely. Now.

"I want you," she murmured as she plied his jaw with kisses. When she reached for the drawstring on his pajamas, he clasped her wrist to stop her.

"Not yet," he told her. "I took my pleasure from giving you yours."

Imogene leaned back and stared at him, incredulous. "I

want to make love with you completely. Not tomorrow or the next day. Tonight.''

Raf smoothed her hair back and kissed her forehead. "I must return to my room now.''

Her frustration escaped on a rough sigh. "Raf, this can't be that great for you. I mean, you haven't even—''

He stopped her with a kiss. "This has been very worthwhile for me. I've never seen you look more beautiful than when you reached your climax. I look forward to the next time. And the next.''

The reality of what they'd done, in front of a mirror no less, hit her hard. Yet that realization didn't temper her need for him. "Don't leave, Raf. Let's finish this now.''

He brought both her hands to his lips and kissed each palm. "This is only the beginning.'' Then he set her aside and stood, his own unanswered need obvious beneath his pajamas.

Holding out his hand, he brought her up into his arms. "Believe me when I say that I want to make love to you, but only when I feel we are ready to take that next step.''

Imogene wanted to hold on to her anger even when she felt as if she might melt against him. "I'm beginning to wonder what you want.''

With a hand on her bottom, he tugged her forward where she could feel the extent of his erection. "You need no longer wonder.''

"Then you're obviously into masochism.''

"I am determined to practice patience.''

"I get that, but why?''

"You will have to trust that my reasons are legitimate.''

"You're obviously determined to make me crazy in the interim.''

"I am determined to make you feel things you have never felt before. To give you pleasure that you've never known with another man.''

He'd already done that. Imogene rested her lips against the middle of his chest. "Tomorrow night, it's going to be my turn."

"I will not be here tomorrow night or the next."

Imogene really wanted to scream now. "Where will you be?"

"In Atlanta. I will be meeting with some prospective investors."

Imogene saw a timely opportunity and went for it. "Maybe I should go with you since you won't be here to give me my lessons."

"Ali, my foreman will see to that in my absence."

"Does that involve only the riding lessons?"

His expression went somber, intense. "He will be instructed to see to your riding only. Aside from that, no one is allowed to touch you but me."

Wow! A regular little macho man. Make that big macho man. But honestly, it thrilled Imogene to see this somewhat possessive side coming out, as long as it only had to do with their lovemaking. "Well, okay, then. If you won't let me go with you, then I'll work really hard while you're gone."

He brought her hands up and kissed each palm. "And when I return, we will continue."

"Promise?"

"You may count on that."

With one last kiss he was gone, and Imogene stood alone in the room, clutching her discarded gown and the strongest sense that she could count on him, no matter what.

She could also fall in love with him.

The thought popped into her brain so quickly, she dropped the gown. Fall in love with him? Ha!

Nope, she couldn't do that. But she very well could. And that would bring regret the likes of which she'd never known. Considering the one devastating mistake she had made with Victoria, the overriding remorse that had stayed with her for years, that was saying quite a bit.

She had too much going on in her life, too much left to accomplish, too many fears driving her to succeed in order to give a man all her time. And she suspected Raf Shakir expected at lot more than she could ever give.

Six

After spending the day touring farms and negotiating, Raf was glad to be back in the hotel suite even though the place seemed stark and lonely. He raked the kaffiyeh off his head and tossed it aside. He rarely wore the headdress but many people believed that since he was a sheikh, he should look the part, though his legacy meant little now. He preferred ragged jeans to royal trappings. However, he would concede comfort for the sake of business. Today had been productive from that standpoint, yet his mind had turned several times to Genie. His strength last night had amazed him. How easy it would have been to work his way into her bed, into her body. Determination had given him that strength, yet it was only a matter of time before that would no longer serve him. He could not resist her much longer, nor did he want to.

As soon as Raf had discarded his tie, the phone rang, generating excitement over the possibility that it could be

Genie. He had gone before dawn without telling her good-bye, but he had left the hotel number on her pillow as well as a kiss on her cheek, fortunately without waking her. If she had come awake and beckoned him into her arms, he would have cancelled this trip. He would have climbed into bed with her and stayed throughout the day until they were both too tired to consider any other activities. Then he would have made love to her again throughout the night.

The phone rang twice more before he drew in a deep breath to restore his composure. "Hello."

"You are very hard to track down, Raf."

The voice was familiar, but it did not belong to Genie. It belonged to his brother. "You've spent most of your adulthood tracking criminals, Darin. I have been in the same place for the past two years."

"Yet you are not there now, which is why I am calling you. I believe it's time you meet my new wife."

"I thought you were traveling throughout the summer."

"We are, but we have decided to pay you a visit en route."

Raf was pleased to hear that news. "As you most likely realize, I am in Atlanta. I will not be returning to the stables until tomorrow."

"As it so happens, we are in Atlanta, as well."

"Where?"

"In the hotel lounge. I thought you might like to join us for a while since we will be departing in the morning."

As exhausted as Raf was, he could not refuse. "I will be there shortly."

"Good. We'll be waiting."

Raf slipped his jacket back on and left the room, arriving in the lobby a short time later. The bar was sparsely pop-ulated and Raf had no trouble spotting the attractive red-haired woman who looked quite small next to his brother. Darin had changed very little since the last time he'd seen

him well over a year ago, with the exception of his notice-
ably shorter hair, something Raf had thought would never
happen. Perhaps his new wife had been responsible for that
change, although he could not imagine Darin allowing a
woman to dictate his choices. Before two months ago, he
could not have imagined Darin married, either.

As Raf drew closer to the table, he saw more subtle
changes, namely Darin's conservative clothing, quite a
transformation from his usual black attire. He also noted
the way Darin smiled at his wife, the way he touched her
possessively, the calm in his expression that had been missing since the death of his beloved fiancée. The intimacy
between the couple was almost tangible and had Raf not
promised to meet them, he would have left the lounge. With
each step he took, his envy escalated, and so did his guilt
over that emotion. After all, Darin had won his hard-earned
peace. Raf should be happy for him. And he was on one
level. On another, he was jealous.

When he arrived at the table, Fiona looked up at him
and smiled. "My gosh, they sure grow the men big in Amythra. I can definitely see the resemblance between you and
Darin."

Darin stood and held out his hand for a shake. "You are
looking well, Raf." He nodded toward his bride. "This is
my wife, Fiona. Fiona, my brother, Raf. He is older but not
necessarily wiser."

Raf shook her hand briefly and took the seat opposite
them. "I am pleased to finally meet the woman who has
ensnared by brother."

"It wasn't that difficult," Fiona said, giving her smile to
Darin. "He may seem tough, but he's really a pushover."

Darin whisked a kiss across her cheek. "I do not remember hearing you complain when I seduced you."

"If my memory serves me correctly, and it does, I seduced you."

Again Raf experienced the sting of envy and he tamped it down with a forced smile. "How long will you be in the States?"

"We leave for Paris in the morning," Darin said. "A belated honeymoon before we settle in Texas permanently."

"A last trip before we're too tied down to travel," Fiona added.

"Darin told me he is building you an inn," Raf said. "I would assume you could eventually hire someone to manage it in your absence should you decide to go abroad again."

Darin and Fiona exchanged a veiled look before Darin said, "We will have something aside from the inn occupying our time in the near future."

Raf did not have to ask, for he could see the pride in Darin's expression. "What would that be?"

Fiona's grin lit up her green eyes, immediately reminding Raf of Genie. "I'm pregnant. I'm really not sure how it happened." Color rose to her face when Darin laughed. "Okay, I know how it happened. It just wasn't supposed to happen quite this soon."

Raf turned his attention to his brother. "I assume you are both happy about this?"

Darin's satisfied expression alone confirmed that fact. "Yes, and we hope that you are happy for us. It's past time for one of us to produce a son."

"Or a girl, which it will be," Fiona said with certainty.

"Of course I am happy for you both, no matter what the child's gender." Raf did well to sound convincing even when he found himself wanting to take his brother's place, but not with Fiona. He did understand why Darin had fallen for this particular woman, but the woman that immediately came to mind had blond hair, a beautiful body and a mind for business—except when it came to lovemaking.

Raf shifted uncomfortably in the rigid chair at the longing that invaded his soul. As fond as he was of Genie, as much as he wanted her, he must continue to remind himself that he would not make the mistake of becoming emotionally involved with a woman who coveted her freedom.

As Darin and Fiona spoke about their new life together, Raf's mood darkened when it should have been joyous. Fortunately, the conversation lasted only an hour before Darin announced they would be retiring for the night, with a knowing look directed at his wife.

They stood at the same time and exchanged parting words and promises to keep in touch. Darin also vowed he would bring Fiona to the farm upon their return to America; Raf said he would try to visit Texas at some time. All in all it was a pleasant enough encounter, even though Raf had battled his own regrets throughout the conversation.

They walked together to the lobby and parted there since Darin and Fiona had taken a room in a different hotel. As Raf entered the elevator, Darin asked, "Who is this Ms. Danforth who told me where to find you? Have you dismissed Doris?"

Raf stopped the doors from closing with his hand. "No. She is not a housekeeper."

Darin smiled. "Is she someone special?"

More than his brother knew. More than Raf had realized. More than she should be. "I am teaching her how to ride."

"I have no doubt about that," Darin said as he sent Fiona a sly smile. "Is she someone we might meet in the future?"

Raf cleared his throat. "She will only be with me for three weeks. This is a business arrangement."

Darin now looked somewhat disappointed. "I was hoping that maybe you had found the right woman." He drove home his point by circling Fiona's waist and pulling her close to his side.

"I will let you know as soon as that happens. If that happens."

Before Darin left, he said, "You never know what the future might hold, brother, as long as you are open to the possibilities."

Raf had considered his future—a future that involved only the stables. Now that future was beginning to look bleak and desolate without someone with whom to share it.

In all the years they had spent together as brothers, tonight was the first time Raf coveted what Darin had—an abiding love with a woman and a child to carry on their legacy.

To Raf that seemed as unattainable as sleep, something he knew would not come easily tonight.

Imogene stared at the phone for a long moment as she muttered a few oaths directed at her cowardice. It was just a friendly call, for Pete's sake. She wasn't going to beg him to come back or cry or even mention that she missed him. She would simply tell him good-night, and give him a good piece of her mind for not bothering to wake her when he'd left that morning.

After picking up the receiver, Imogene pounded out the number he'd left on the pillow that morning, before she changed her mind. She only had to wait a few minutes for the hotel operator to connect her to his room. After three rings, she almost hung up until she heard his incredible voice greeting her with a simple "Hello" that nearly knocked her off the edge of the mattress.

"And hello to you. Did you have fun today?"

"I would not consider it fun, but you could say it was fruitful."

"Good. I missed you." Oh, jeez. Did she really just say that? "Ali isn't nearly as grouchy as you are." Good save,

Imogene. "Guess I like being bossed around more than I realized."

"I did warn him about your stubbornness. I hope that when I return, he will still be in my employ."

That would have made Imogene mad had his tone not been teasing. "I'll have you know, I was a model student. And I had a nice conversation with your brother. Did he reach you?"

"Yes. He joined me earlier with his new wife. I had not met her until tonight."

"What was she like?"

"A very nice woman. They are expecting a child."

The wistfulness in Raf's voice took Imogene back. She couldn't imagine Raf Shakir pining for a family, but then she couldn't imagine a lot of things about him and so far he'd surprised her at several turns. "That's great. I'm sure you're looking forward to being an uncle."

"Where are you now?" he asked, his voice impossibly lower than before.

"I'm in my bedroom, sitting on the bed."

"Are you wearing red?"

All over her body. "Actually, I'm wearing blue pajamas. What are you wearing?"

"Nothing."

She could picture that in great detail, except for one very important detail and only because she hadn't seen that part of him. She could visualize it, though, and that excited her. "Do you always sleep in the nude?"

"For the most part. How is your sunburn?"

"Much better, thank you."

"Have you looked in the mirror tonight?"

Her gaze zeroed in on said mirror before she collapsed onto the bed. "Considering it covers one wall, it's kind of hard to avoid it."

"Did you see us together? What we did last night?"

In two more minutes, Imogene was going to strip out of her own clothes lest they catch fire from the heat of his words. "I doubt I'll ever forget it."

"Keep it in your thoughts and remember, what we've done is only the beginning. I will see you evening after next, if all goes as planned. Good night, Genie."

Before she had enough presence of mind to say good-night, the line went dead, but Imogene's body immediately came to life. She rolled onto her belly and smashed her face in the pillow to muffle her shout. All she needed was to have Doris hurrying into the room, believing Imogene was being attacked by some shifty intruder who'd managed to scale the wall and come in through the balcony door. She was under attack all right—a sensual attack facilitated by a man who could make her shiver with only the sound of his voice. And when he did return, if he lived up to his promise, she hoped she survived what else he intended to do with her, to her.

In the meantime, she planned a few surprises of her own, beginning tomorrow morning. With Ali as her coconspirator, she would prove to Raf that she could get this whole horse thing right.

When they reached SaHráa, Raf instructed his driver to let him out at the stables. Normally he would go into the house and change into his work clothes but he did not want to wait another minute. Not after he caught sight of Genie riding Maurice in the arena.

He shirked off his tie, coat and kaffiyeh, leaving them behind in the car before he exited. As he strode toward the arena, he released the top button of his tailored shirt to give him more air since the sight of Genie greatly hindered his breathing. She looked magnificent in the saddle with wisps of golden hair surrounding her face, her chin tipped up with pride, her perfect body in perfect form.

Raf moved to the gate and braced one foot on the bottom rung, looking his fill before she noticed him.

"You may proceed now," Ali said from the center of the pen.

Genie walked a few strides before cuing Maurice into the trot. Shock and concern sent Raf forward to throw open the gate and stalk inside. "I will take it from here," he told Ali who looked perplexed by Raf's acid tone.

"As you wish, Your Excellency." Ali left the arena the moment Genie rounded the pen. She glanced at Ali first, seeming confused by his departure until she spotted Raf.

When their gazes met, she pulled Maurice to a stop and smiled. "You're back! Watch this."

The anger he had effectively kept in check over the past two years settled heavily on Raf as Genie again trotted the gelding, posting in the saddle with an expertise he had not expected.

He should have been present for this milestone. He should have been the one to teach her. For a brief, irrational moment he wondered what else Ali had shown her. An absurd thought, considering the man was almost sixty and happily married to his wife, Fatinah, for well over thirty years. They had borne six children, all grown now, and if Raf looked at it logically, he could not imagine Ali having enough energy left to bed a younger woman.

Raf must be insane for even assuming such a thing. He also grew painfully hard as he continued to watch Genie's hips rising and falling on the saddle as she continued to post, spurring thoughts of another instance where she could do to the same with him. The pressure was almost as unbearable as the heat from the sun and the fire she was generating. That desperate need for her only served to fuel his anger.

The loss of control brought about his scowl when she

guided Maurice into the center of the pen and dismounted like a professional. "So what do you think?" she asked.

Raf could not think, could not reason with his mind clouded by a mesh of emotions he could not begin to understand. "I think you are finished for the day." He spun around and headed into the stables, leaving Genie gaping in the middle of the pen.

When Raf walked into the barn, he found Ali standing in the aisle, looking somewhat disapproving. He strode into Maurice's stall and pretended to check the hay.

"Are you displeased with the progress Miss Danforth has made?" Ali said through the iron bars separating the stall from the aisle.

"She is not ready."

"Forgive me, but I believe you've seen evidence to the contrary. She is quite a natural rider."

"My only concern is her safety. I do not want her progressing too quickly."

"She is moving at a pace that suits her abilities."

Raf could hear the clip-clop of Maurice's lazy gait and Genie's faster footsteps approaching. "Ali, take the gelding and rinse him off, then you are dismissed."

Ali met Genie at the entrance and took Maurice from her. Raf could hear their muttered conversation and he assumed they were discussing him. It did not matter. He had to escape before he did something foolish or said something regrettable.

Raf left the stall and started up the aisle, hoping that Genie would not pursue him yet assuming she probably would.

"Wait up, Raf," she called as he ascended the stairs to the apartment, confirming his assumptions.

He did not answer her or slow his steps, but he could not avoid her when she followed him into the apartment.

"Raf, stop running from me, dammit!" she said as he entered the office.

He faced the shelves positioned behind his desk, determined not to look at her. "What do you wish from me? My congratulations when you've so blatantly ignored my wishes?"

"I learned to trot. Big deal. Why does that make you so angry?"

"I am angry at Ali. I told him that you were to walk only."

"Don't blame him. I'm the one who convinced him to let me trot."

"He works for me, not you."

"Would you just look at me for a minute?"

He did not dare, for if he did, he would most likely let go of his anger. He needed that emotion, otherwise he would disregard common sense and take her into his arms to vent his frustration, his all-consuming need for her. "I have some work to do before dinner. I prefer to be alone."

"I'm not leaving until I find out what this is really all about."

Raf turned to find her expression a mix of confusion and irritation. "This is about not following my directives. You could have been injured."

"I'm still in one piece."

He could not resist taking a long glance down her body. "As luck would have it, yes, you are."

She crossed her arms over her chest, shielding her breasts from his eyes. "It has nothing to do with luck. Ali is a great teacher."

Raf experienced another spear of anger. "Then perhaps he should take over for me, if I am not meeting your needs."

"I don't want him to teach me, I want you to do it, but—"

"Yet you refused to adhere to our agreement."

"Yes, but—"

"And I believe I said that if you made that decision, then our arrangement would be nullified, did I not?"

"Yes, you did—"

"So is that what you want, Genie? Do you want to call off this arrangement?"

"No, that's not what I want. I just want you to listen to me. I wanted to prove to myself that I could do it." Her gaze drifted away. "I did it for you."

For him? His anger slowly dissolved. He had been responsible for destroying her sense of accomplishment. He had let his own guilt and fears influence him. "Why would you need my approval?"

She dropped her arms to her sides. "Because it's important to me. I thought you would be proud, but obviously I was wrong."

"I am disappointed that you did not wait until my return to take the next step in your lessons. Now that you have done that, I have no choice but to accept it."

"But you're not happy about it, are you?"

He could not begin to express what he felt at that moment—anger, regret, desire. *Fear.* Fear of his feelings for her, fear that he could easily let emotions rule logic. "I am frustrated."

"Frustrated about what, Raf?" She closed the space between them until she stood very close. "Does this really have to do with me defying you? Or are you frustrated because you want me, and for some reason that scares you?"

"I am not afraid of you."

"Really? Then prove it."

Raf's tenuous control snapped and he spun her around, backing her up against the shelves. He framed her face in his palms, forcing her to look at him, to know what she had unleashed. "You have no idea what you are doing to me. For the past two nights I have stayed awake for hours thinking about you until I was so hard I could not sleep. And today, watching you ride, I still wanted you, even though I was furious to find you had ignored my mandates."

She slid her hands up his chest and brought them to rest on his shoulders. "Then you must be really tired."

Taking her hand, he guided her palm down his chest past his abdomen and pressed it against his erection. "This is not a result of exhaustion."

He should have known she would not draw her hand away. He did not realize she would release his belt and unfasten the button on his slacks. With effort, Raf clasped her wrist to stop her. "No."

"Yes." She wrested her hand from his grasp and lowered his fly.

He should put an end to this, but he could not muster enough strength. "I have nothing here to protect you from pregnancy."

"That's not an issue because I am protected against pregnancy."

"Are you not concerned about other issues of safety?"

"Should I be?"

"No."

"Good. But this isn't about me," she said, searching his eyes as she lowered his briefs. "This is about you. It's my turn now to give back what you've given me."

Several protests worked their way into Raf's mind but dispersed the moment she freed him and took him into her hand. He tipped his forehead against hers and lowered his gaze to watch, too lost to stop her. Too overwhelmed by the sensations to do anything but immerse himself in the moment.

Many years had passed since a woman had touched him

this way. Daliya never had. Perhaps no one ever had, at least not with such thorough persuasion, such selflessness that she would want to tend to his needs without considering her own.

He planned to remedy that. "I want to touch you." When he reached for the clasp on her pants, she pulled his hand back to her waist.

"This is just for you, Raf," she whispered. "You need this. I need to do this. So let go and enjoy it. I plan to."

He gritted his teeth as she increased the pressure and cadence of her strokes, firm milking strokes that had his hips following her movements as he leaned into her. He needed to end this before it was too late. He needed to wait until he was inside her. Yet he did not have the will to stop. She had no idea how much power she had over him at that moment. No idea that he would have gladly relinquished his fortune for the opportunity to feel this good again, to experience this freedom.

He could no longer think beyond the force of his impending climax. Blessed relief was within reach, yet he wanted the sensations to last. A long breath hissed from between his clenched teeth as he battled his body's demand. He fought to hold on. But it had been too long since he had felt this way. Perhaps never this way.

All sound disappeared save for the incessant pounding of his pulse in his ears and his ragged breathing. Every muscle in his body went rigid as an explosive climax burst forth, nearly collapsing him with its power. In one long, mind-shattering moment, two years of self-imposed celibacy ended in the hands of a woman who moved him in so many ways.

All the emotions crowding in on him—relief, gratitude, longing—came out in a kiss heralding his desperation. She accepted all that he gave, willingly opened to him and drew his tongue deep into the welcome heat of her mouth. And he had given her nothing but grief, while she had given him the sweetest, most unselfish gift of pleasure in its purest form.

Remorse caused Raf to break the kiss and step back. Emotionally and physically drained, he redid his fly and dropped into the nearby chair, his head in his hands, his heart in turmoil.

He was mildly aware of the sound of the closing bathroom door adjacent to the office. He was very aware when Genie returned and dropped to her knees before him. He raised his gaze to hers, knowing she could see through his attempts to mask his emotions when she said, "It's okay. There's nothing wrong with what just happened."

"Yet you received nothing in return."

She laid a gentle hand on his jaw. "Oh, but I did. I got to see you give up some of your control for a change. I got to see you when you feel as good as you made me feel. At least I'm hoping it felt good."

Much more than she could fathom. "I wanted to wait until we made love. It was important to me."

"Why was that so important? You needed that release and I wanted to be the one to give it to you."

He came to his feet and stared down on her. "And I wanted you to be the one to give it to me as well, but not this way." Before he could halt the words, they came tumbling out of his mouth. "You are the *only* woman I have allowed to be this close to me again. The only woman I have been with in two years. That is why it was important."

Raf did not wait to see her reaction before he left the room, knowing he would probably regret the revelation. With that information, more questions would come. Questions he was not certain he wanted to answer, for with them would also come the knowledge that he was not the man Genie Danforth presumed him to be.

Seven

*You are the only woman I have allowed to be this close to
me again. The only woman I have been with in two years....*

Even after two days, Imogene still reeled from the revelation. Why her? Why now? And what had been the cause
of his withdrawal from life?

She had so many unanswered questions. So many things
she wanted to know about Raf Shakir. Since their interlude
in the barn, she hadn't seen him aside from lessons, and
those had been attended by both Raf and Ali. Safety in
numbers, Imogene decided. She also decided that what
she'd done to him might have been a critical mistake. She
wasn't exactly sorry she'd done it even though it had been
a first for her. But to see Raf that vulnerable, to know she
had been responsible for giving him the pleasure he'd given
to her, to see him let down his guard, had almost been
worth it. Or it would have been if he hadn't continued to
avoid her.

She got the distinct feeling that any chance of making love with him could be nil. Even so, she had to know what had happened in his life that had made him so sad, made him close himself off from life so effectively that he'd not been with a woman for two years. She could very much relate to that sadness because of her own experience, but she hadn't totally checked out of life, even if she had used her job as a means to escape.

Raf wouldn't be the one to give her the answers, that much Imogene knew. She decided to join Doris in the kitchen after dining alone again, hoping that maybe she could persuade the housekeeper to give up some more information.

Making her way to the high-top counter, she slid onto a stool while Doris swiped a rag over the surface, literally whistling ''Dixie'' while she worked.

''So what does the sheikh do on a normal Saturday night?'' she asked. ''Play poker with the guys?''

Doris turned and leaned back against the stove. ''He's not the poker-playing kind, even if he does have a poker face.''

''How do you mean?''

''You should know by now that he hides his feelings.''

Imogene did know, all too well. ''So have you seen him this evening?'' She kept her tone light to conceal her curiosity.

''He was in here right before dinner to get some coffee. Looks like the mare they've been waiting on to foal might domino tonight. I told those boys that a watched pot never boils. My husband stared at me for two weeks when I was expecting my first so I waited until he left to go fishing before I went into labor.'' Doris threw back her head and cackled, then threw down the rag. ''I got him good on that one.''

Imogene rested her cheek on her palm. "I didn't know you were married and had children."

"I've got three boys living in all parts of the country with their wives and a whole slew of grandkids. I've been hitched for almost forty years now, not that Bernie Blaylock remembers it's been that long."

Surprise straightened Imogene in her seat. "You're married to Mr. Blaylock?"

Doris looked altogether confused. "Why, yes, sugar, I am. We live in one of the houses on the grounds, next door to Ali and his wife. Didn't His Majesty tell you that?"

"Nope. The sheikh isn't too forthcoming with information."

"I meant my husband. I like to call him His Majesty because I've been cleaning his throne since the beginning of time." Again Doris released a round of grinding chuckles. Imogene might have laughed, too, but at the moment, she wasn't in a jovial mood.

She decided now was the time to grab the opportunity to quiz Doris a little about the other "majesty." "Did Sheikh Shakir have any children when he was married?"

"No, sugar, no kiddos. They were only married a short time before…" Doris abruptly turned back to the stove. "I swear, grease just goes forth and multiplies after I fry chicken."

Determination sent Imogene from the bar stool. She walked to the stove and leaned one hip against the counter next to Doris. "They were married a short time before what?"

Doris offered Imogene only a brief glance before going back to working the stove over with a vengeance. "I've said too much already. If you want to know, you'll have to ask him about it."

"He won't tell me."

Doris turned to face her with a sympathetic look. "Then let it be, sugar. Some things are best left unsaid."

In some instances Imogene would heartily agree. After all, she rarely spoke about the night Tori had disappeared. But this time she was driven by her burgeoning feelings for Raf to find out more, before she was in too deep. She was already in too deep.

"Can you at least tell me how long it's been since his marriage ended?" she asked.

Doris attacked another burner with the cloth. "He came to Georgia right after..." Her hand and words hesitated simultaneously. "Right after he wasn't married anymore. That's been two years ago."

Obviously the end of his marriage had devastated him enough to keep him away from any intimacy. Again, Imogene questioned why Raf had chosen her to end his celibacy. Probably because she was simply available and in some ways, non-threatening. He knew she didn't plan to stay beyond three weeks, less if Sid had his way. When her time with Raf was over, then they would be, too. No strings attached. No long-term commitment. That was okay with Imogene. After all, she still had her career. So why did she feel so down in the dumps?

Deciding Doris was probably quite done with the revelations, Imogene patted the woman on the back and smiled. "Do you think 'the boys' would mind if I join them? I've never seen a horse being born."

Doris's wily grin returned. "Land sakes, girl, you are green as new mold. What are you doing on a horse farm?"

"Trying to learn how to ride." Trying not to fall in love with her teacher.

Doris clucked her tongue. "That may have been your original reason for being here, but something tells me you've found another reason to stay."

The woman was just too darned intuitive, or Imogene

was too darned obvious. "I can't stay because I have a job to do. In fact, work is piling up while I'm standing here talking to you."

Doris faced Imogene, a knowing look on her heart-shaped face. "Work won't keep you warm at night, sugar. Just ask the sheikh when you get a chance. Of course, he's not going to admit that, either."

Imogene assumed that much, but at least she could try. First, she had to find him and eventually get him alone.

Imogene finally found the foaling barn by process of elimination and following the sound of muffled voices. She entered to discover Ali and Mr. Blaylock standing in the aisle.

When Imogene approached them, Blaylock removed his cap and Ali nodded. Raf was crouched in the corner of the oversize stall, elbows resting on his knees, hands clasped together. All three men looked totally engrossed in observing the mare lying on her side, her ribs rising and falling with each ragged breath she drew.

"Should I call the vet now?" Ali asked.

Raf raised a hand. "Not yet. Ali, you may go home to your wife. Blaylock, do the same but have Doris put on some coffee. This could take a while."

Imogene took that as her cue to leave, since Raf hadn't acknowledged her presence, but as she started away behind the men, she heard him say, "Genie, stay."

She headed back down the aisle while the others kept walking. Once she reached the stall, she stared at Raf through the bars, afraid she hadn't heard correctly. "Did you say something to me?"

He sent her a quick glance before bringing his attention back to the mare. "Come inside and keep me company. Please."

He didn't have to ask her twice. Imogene lifted the latch,

opened the door and quietly entered. "Where do you want me?"

A smile played along his mouth but didn't quite form. "Next to me."

Imogene complied, lowering herself to her knees yet leaving a comfortable distance between her and Raf. She was touched that he had asked her to stay. Thrilled that he would want her sharing in this moment. And still so drawn to him that just seeing him dressed in his standard denim jeans, frayed at the hem where they covered his scuffed boot heels, the denim shirt rolled up to the elbows, stole her breath.

Comfortable silence settled over the stall, broken only by the mare's occasional whinny. "How long do you think before it will happen?" Imogene finally asked.

"Soon," Raf said.

"How long has she been like this?"

"A few hours."

"And she doesn't need a vet?"

"No. This is her tenth foal. She tends to take her time. She will deliver when she is ready."

"What's her name?"

"Jasmine, but her official name is—"

"Never mind. I'll just call her Jasmine." Right now Imogene would rather call her stubborn.

While they continued to observe, the mare stood twice and lifted her tail, then settled back on the ground. The seconds turned into minutes, minutes into two hours, and still she didn't appear as if she had any intention of having a baby.

Imogene's legs began to cramp so she plopped down on her bottom, knees bent where she rested her arms. At least the shavings were clean and smelled of fresh-cut wood. She glanced at Raf who was still crouching, surprised his thighs had been able to maintain that position for as long as they had. No denying it, Raf Shakir had strong, solid thighs. He also had the most fantastic, well-defined forearms covered in a fine veneer of warm skin and masculine hair. His hands were also solid and strong and large, his fingers square and blunt. She trembled when she remembered how he had used them on her so methodically, sensually.

"Are you cold?"

Imogene looked up from his hands, only then realizing that she'd been caught staring and shivering. "No. I'm fine."

"Would you like to return to the house? It is getting late."

She didn't want to be away from him for a moment, even if it meant sitting on a barn floor waiting for Jasmine, who seemed determined not to accommodate them. "I wouldn't dare leave now. I just know if I do, she'll have that baby and I would've missed the whole thing."

"Have you ever seen a foal's birth before?"

"No. In fact, I've never seen anything being born."

"It is something not to be missed. Truly a miracle. It is not often we have the chance to experience it in our lifetime."

It was a miracle that Imogene didn't kiss him, even though she dearly wanted to. "I'm willing to wait." Wait for the mare. Wait to once more know the pleasure of Raf's kiss. She was determined to know that, and more. Maybe even someday she might understand his enigmatic soul.

The mare snorted as if she believed that to be a long shot at best. Or maybe she wished they would leave and let her labor in peace. Then she lifted her head and nipped at her sides, drawing Imogene's attention to the discernible roll in her belly. "I can see it moving," she said. "That's incredible."

"And you will soon see it come into this world."

Raf was right. The first signs of life appeared in the form

of two spindly legs emerging, then a nose that looked as if it were attached to those legs. After a few more attempts at pushing, the baby arrived completely. The mare hopped up, snapping the umbilical cord, then proceeded to remove the sac covering the foal's face and body. The baby's damp coat was black as the cloud-covered night surrounding them. Raf, who had finally stood, announced that Jasmine had given birth to a filly.

Imogene came to her feet and watched Raf wipe the foal's body with a towel, exercising as much care as he had shown her when he'd touched her. After struggling and falling twice, the baby finally rose up on shaky legs and staggered toward her mother.

Imogene laughed when the foal's tiny lips began to work as she instinctively searched for her first meal. She grew silent when Raf came up behind her and wrapped his arms around her waist, pulling her close against his chest.

As they watched the filly nurse then settle in to sleep at her mother's feet, Imogene experienced total contentment. She supposed new life had a way of bringing about optimism, but that wasn't the only thing lifting her heart and spirits. The connection that she and Raf had in those moments was intangible but it felt so real. She could go on this way for hours, secure in his arms while playing witness to this wonder.

"She is perfect," Raf said, his tone almost reverent.

"Yes, she is. BáHar should be proud of his firstborn." She looked back at Raf. "Speaking of that, you're going to make a great father some day."

She saw a flicker of that same old sadness in his eyes. "If that opportunity ever arises."

Imogene decided to take a risk, one that she hoped would pay off. "Did you and your wife want children?"

His arms stiffened, a sure sign he was raising an emotional wall. "How did you know about my wife?"

"I inadvertently found out you were married at one time. But I don't know why you aren't married now."

"I prefer to keep the past in the past." His voice sounded flat and emotionless, as if he had totally withdrawn, splintering their special time together.

Imogene considered an apology for being so intrusive but she didn't want to make matters worse. At least he hadn't released her or walked away.

But she realized their time had come to an end when Raf dropped his arms from around her. "You should go to bed now since it's past midnight. You need to be rested for our morning lesson."

Imogene turned and witnessed the impassive mask he used to effectively screen his emotions. "Just a few more minutes. I want to make sure I remember all the details." She couldn't stand the thought of leaving him, either, but he was determined to dismiss her, apparent when he unlatched the door and opened it.

"You may have pictures to take with you when you leave here," he said.

That served as another reminder that eventually Imogene would have to leave this place, and him. She would have to return to the real world of high finance and long hours. If she didn't get a grip on her feelings for Raf, it would be much too hard to leave when the time came. He was unreachable, untouchable, at least when it came to the business of his heart.

On that thought, she left the stall. "I'll see you in the morning," she said without looking back. She didn't want Raf to see her disappointment. She didn't want to run back into his arms and make a total fool of herself. If he wanted to take up where they'd left off, then it would have to be up to him.

Imogene would simply go to bed and grab a few hours of sleep, be up in the morning raring to go and forget the fact that she wanted more than anything to have him beside her for what remained of the night—and if things were different, what remained of her life.

Shortly before dawn, Raf braced his arm on the door frame and watched Genie sleep. Only moments ago he'd come to her room, intending only to tell her she could remain in bed longer since the weather was not cooperating this Saturday morning. But the sight of her curled on her side wearing only a sheer white camisole that conformed to her breasts and a pair of satin shorts had left him unable to turn away.

Although she looked peaceful with one hand resting next to her face, the sheet was crumpled at the end of the bed as if she had struggled with it during the night, the same as Raf had struggled with his feelings for her. The way he struggled now with the undeniable craving to make love with her.

Yet he was uncertain if she would want him in her bed after their most recent conversation. He should have issued an apology, explained why he did not wish to discuss his past. Instead, he had dismissed Genie in order to avoid her questions and his own underlying guilt.

He lingered in the doorway, knowing she would be warm and as soft as fine silk if he touched her. He should leave her be, allow her to rest and take the day off from his demands. Yet he could not leave her because of what she was doing to him—body and soul.

How much longer could he go on this way, desperately wanting and needing her, yet fearing he needed her too much? How long could he continue to deny himself or her? No longer. This time he would not turn away from her. He would give her his best. Everything. Completely.

Raf closed the door and locked it behind him, slipped out of his jeans and briefs and crossed to the end of the bed. He worked his way up the mattress, fitted himself against Genie's back and slid his hand down her arm while he brushed his lips over her shoulder. He took those moments to memorize the feel of her skin, to relish the scent of her hair, the warmth of her body.

She finally roused when he kissed her neck. Her eyes fluttered open and she looked back at him with an unfocused gaze. "Why—"

He pressed his fingertip to her lips. "We have no need for words. We have better ways to spend our time."

She rolled onto her back and stretched. Realization dawned in her expression as she palmed his unshaven jaw and lifted her head to kiss his lips chastely, yet it served to encourage him.

Pulling Genie up until she sat before him, Raf clasped the hem of the camisole and worked it over her head, then tossed it aside. He took a few moments simply to hold her, to explore the smooth plane of her spine with his palms, to take pleasure in her breasts fitted against his chest. Gliding his hands through her hair, he held her in place for a kiss. As always she opened to him, met the play of his tongue with her own. He drew away and sipped at her lips before entering her mouth again and again.

After guiding her back onto the bed, he paused to study her emerald eyes. She contemplated him as if she sensed how monumental these moments would be. How long he had waited for this—since the day she had walked into his life.

Lowering his mouth to her breasts, he suckled her until he felt the movement of her hips beneath him, knowing she needed much more. And he would endeavor to give it to her.

He gradually inched her shorts down, leaving kisses on her bare flesh in their wake. When he had them worked below her navel, he sat up and pulled the garment completely away to reveal she wore nothing underneath, serving to heighten his desire.

He slid both hands up her bare thighs and back down again, bent her knees then nudged them apart to make a place for himself. He heard the catch of Genie's breath, and he hesitated. He would first make certain she wanted this intimacy and if she did, there would be no turning back until he had given her the ultimate pleasure.

Resting his cheek on her thigh, he sifted his fingers through the golden down between her legs and watched her face. He only saw anticipation in her expression, then acquiescence when her eyes drifted closed.

"Watch what I do to you, Genie," he whispered.

She responded by opening her eyes, pure, persuasive desire reflecting from them. Only then did Raf skim her warm flesh with his tongue. Genie's hips lifted toward him, not away, encouraging him to be more ardent, and he was, with every insistent stroke of his tongue, every steady tug of his lips, every gentle push of his finger inside her.

He looked up to see that she had turned her face toward the mirror to observe, and he pressed his palm on her thigh to nudge her leg straight, offering her an unencumbered view, believing it would serve to intensify her pleasure as well as his own. His body burned when he felt the beginning waves of her climax, when he watched in the mirror's reflection the moment it overtook her. He slid two fingers inside her so that he could feel what she experienced. And he intended to feel it again when he was deep inside her body.

She murmured his name, and Raf recognized the sound of gratification and absolute pleasure in her voice, knowing she was ready to take the final step. He worked his way back up her abdomen with more kisses and, through sheer will alone, refrained from plunging into her. Instead he kissed her with temperance, demonstrating with his tongue what he would soon accomplish when he crossed the boundary between wanting and having.

''I want all of you,'' she whispered, the only words she had spoken, yet exactly what Raf needed to hear as fervently as he needed to be inside her.

''And you will have me.'' All that he could give.

The steady succession of raindrops pelting the roof and the distant sound of thunder were the only sounds disturbing the quiet. Yet Raf's heart pounded against his chest as he guided himself to her, knowing hc balanced at the point of achieving this long-awaited reward.

As he drew in a cleansing breath, he pushed inside Genie's body, ending his lonely existence devoid of intimacy. He exhaled a long breath of satisfaction and remained very still to savor the sensations of her body sheathing his, until he could wait no longer. He found Genie's mouth again at the same time he claimed the rhythm his body required. He alternated between kissing her lips and her breasts as he lifted her hips with his palms, creating the friction she would need to bring about another climax. The heaviness gathered between his legs, the heat consumed him as Genie met him, thrust for thrust. He wanted to slow down to make the moment last, yet he would not deprive her of her own fulfillment. And only moments following her orgasm, Raf let go as he had never let go before.

He buried his face in her hair fanning out on the pillow as he tensed with the climax, inside and out. His hands shook as did his body from the onslaught of overpowering sensations. Never before had he reacted so strongly with a woman. Never before had he wanted so much.

Once his respiration had calmed, Raf rolled to his side and enfolded her in his arms. Again no words passed between them, only gentle touches, soft caresses over arms and shoulders and backs as if they were starved for the contact. In many ways, Raf was.

The knowledge that Genie had accepted him voluntarily gave him the peace that had evaded him until now. She continued to hold him as if providing an anchor against the storm raging outside the house and inside his soul. Soothed by the warmth of her body, by the calm he now felt, he gave in to his exhaustion and slept with her in his arms.

Eight

Imogene stood at the French doors and watched the oaks bowing to the strong winds and the lines of horizontal rain. But the weather's wrath hadn't awakened her. Once again Tori had appeared to her in the persistent dream, but unlike before, this time she'd spoken.

Don't give up, Genie.

Imogene had awakened with a start, shaking, her face shrouded in tears that she didn't want Raf to see, the reason why she'd left their bed. She tightened her robe about her but that did little to alleviate the chills. Only Raf could provide the warmth she now needed.

She sensed his presence before he wrapped his arms around her waist to tug her back against him. His lips were soft against her neck, his hands gentle as he ran one lightly over her breast.

"I did not like waking to find you had left me," he said, his voice a rough growl. "Was it the storm?"

She decided to settle for a half truth. "It's almost noon. I don't normally lie around this long, doing nothing."

"You consider what we've done nothing?"

She turned into his arms, thankful to find a smile not anger on his beautiful face. She ruffled his already tousled hair. "You know what I mean. I can't remember the last time I really took a day off. I went from high school to college, obtained my MBA while interning. And then I moved right into a competitive career in a coveted job that kicks my butt on a regular basis."

"And you still enjoy this job?"

She shrugged. "Guess I'm into self-torture." He had no idea how much truth there was in that statement. Or maybe he did. "Besides, this job is only a stepping stone. I have much bigger plans for my future."

He scrutinized her with eyes a close match to the skies outside. "Is your job the only thing that is troubling you?"

Raf's uncanny knack at reading her continually surprised Imogene. Maybe she should tell him what had been bothering her. Maybe if she did, he would be more inclined to open up to her. God knew, she wanted that more than anything now. "I had a dream about my little sister. That's what woke me."

"A nightmare?"

"A five-year nightmare. She's been gone that long."

He tightened his hold on her. "What became of her?"

Imogene took a deep draw of air and let it out slowly, preparing to talk about the horrible episode in her life with the only person she'd ever confided in outside the family. "She went to a concert in Atlanta and she never returned home. Vanished without a trace."

"Did she run away?"

Imogene shook her head. "No. She wouldn't do that. Even if she had gotten it in her head to do something like that, she would have eventually called me. We were very close. She's the one who called me 'Genie' first. And I'm responsible for her disappearance.''

He frowned. ''How are you responsible?''

She wasn't too sure she could confess with him staring at her expectantly, but she would if it meant he might eventually open up to her. ''It was Victoria's seventeenth birthday. I was supposed to go to the concert with her, but I was too busy trying to keep afloat so I could get ahead. I can't help thinking that if I'd been there, I might have prevented it from happening.''

''Or perhaps you might have fallen victim, as well.''

Imogene stiffened in his arms. ''She's not dead, Raf. I know this sounds crazy, but I can feel her presence. In the dream she told me not to give up, and I won't. I can't.''

He drew her against his solid chest and stroked her hair. ''Nor should you give up hope if that gives you peace.''

The regret in his tone led Imogene to believe he did understand her pain. And she wanted to know why. ''What do you hope for, Raf?'' she asked, seeking his eyes in order to weigh his reaction.

He pushed her bangs aside and left a kiss on her forehead. ''I hope that you will be willing to come back to bed with me so that we can do nothing for the rest of the day and well into the night.''

It was obvious to Imogene he still wasn't going to bare his soul. But that was okay since he had at least bared his gorgeous body. One obvious part of him had come fully awake, and she was lost to him again.

She ran her hands over the curve of his bare bottom. ''I can't think of anything better than spending the day under the covers with you.''

Taking her totally by surprise, he swept her off her feet, at which time the robe drifted away along with Imogene's tenuous hold on her heart. He laid her down carefully on the mattress and kissed her thoroughly, tenderly. He touched her again, first whispering words of consolation then words of seduction that made her want him all the more. Made her want to love him. And with every ragged breath she drew, with every rapid beat of her heart, she did.

For the next few days Imogene was caught in a surreal web of carnal pleasure at the hands of Raf Shakir. He now knew every inch of her body, and she knew his, had explored it without inhibitions with her fingertips and her mouth. She'd learned to voice her own desires and he'd had no qualms about telling her what he liked and where he wanted to be touched.

He'd been insatiable, but then so had she. He'd grown more brazen to the point Imogene never knew exactly when or where they would make love. She'd told him about her love-in-the-horse-stall fantasy, and he'd made that a reality one afternoon in broad daylight with their bodies slick from the hot, summer sun, running the risk that they might be caught even though they'd kept on most of their clothes. One evening following dinner and Doris's departure, they had fondled each other beneath the table, both so hot and needy that they'd never made it beyond the stairs before he'd made love to her on the landing.

He had shown her every form of pleasure imaginable—and some she hadn't begun to imagine—in front of the mirror. Needless to say, she would never look at her reflection in the same way again. She would never look at lovemaking the same way either. He was spoiling her with his mastery, and stealing her heart with every lovely interlude.

But at night, in the quiet aftermath of their lovemaking, when they had talked about their day, when she'd witnessed his inherent gentleness in his voice when he spoke her name, when he'd held her until the first signs of dawn, those were the times she would cherish most. Those were the moments when she'd known he was a man she could love for all time and probably would, regardless of what the future held.

But as Raf had grown more liberal with his affections, Sid had grown more impatient with Imogene's absence. She'd taken to carrying her phone with her at all times, even during lessons, in case he called. She tried appeasing him in order to buy a little more time at the stables. He'd been all for Imogene striking a deal with Raf regarding his syndication, but that hadn't been enough to subdue his threats about finding a replacement for her if she didn't get back to the office.

Today Imogene pushed all those concerns out of her mind. Raf had promised to take her to the next step in her lessons. She'd assumed that meant she would be riding Maurice, but as she approached the arena, she found Raf sitting atop BáHar, sans saddle, the gelding nowhere in sight.

She stared up at him—a dark, arresting image against the blue, blue sky. Today the wind was strong, blowing his hair back from his face and complementing Imogene's topsy-turvy emotions. Every time she looked at him, her heart took a skid. Every time she considered the limited number of days before her departure, depression settled over her. But because she had so little time left, she refused to spend it moping around. To do anything less than value each moment with him would be completely counterproductive.

She laid a hand on his thigh, a sure sign of the intimacy that now existed between them. "Where's my mount?"

"I would like to show you something before we begin our lesson."

Imogene grinned. "I'm sure you would, but I thought you were going to show me how to canter."

"I will in a while. First, we ride together."

When he held out his hand for Imogene, she started to issue a protest, to insist that she needed the lesson badly if she was ever going to pull this whole client thing off. But when he continued to study her with his powerful gray eyes, all her arguments fled.

Raf took her hand and lifted her up with little effort, positioning her in front of him, the same as he had the first time they'd ridden this way almost two weeks ago. But this time Imogene was so much more comfortable, both with Raf and the horse.

They took off at a walk down a path past the paddock where Jasmine grazed on lush grass, the yet-to-be-named filly that Imogene called Sassy running circles around the mare. Open pasture soon gave way to a thicket that nearly blocked the sun.

As Raf guided the horse forward through the woods, Imogene leaned back against him to enjoy the leisurely ride. They hadn't gone far before he managed to find his way to the drawstring on her wind pants that she'd worn instead of the breeches. She'd thought it odd that he hadn't commented on the attire. Now she knew why.

"You're a bad boy, Raf," she said as he slowly untied the string.

"You did not say that last night outside on the verandah." He slid his hand beneath the pants and traced the lace band on her panties with one fingertip.

"Last night it was late and dark and—" Any attempts at further protest escaped her when he inched a little lower, this time below the satin.

"Yes, Genie?" He sounded amused, but his caress was deadly. Deadly to her senses, to her sense of reality. The pulse pounding in her ears drove away the afternoon sounds as he teased her with his arousing touch, tempted her with his evocative words, propelling her into a world of uninhibited pleasure.

Lost to him once more, Imogene managed a broken breath and a halfhearted scolding. "I swear, Raf, I'm going to…"

"Yes, I believe you are."

And she did, shuddering over the climax he was capable of giving her with such little effort.

Imogene no longer recognized the woman she had become under his expert guidance. A woman who only now realized what she had been missing while going about the business of day-to-day living. A woman totally captivated by a man who treated her as if fulfilling her desires, her fantasies, held more importance than anything in his life. Even if she spent years searching for this experience with another man, she wouldn't be successful. And she probably would never find anyone who came close to being his equal. Maybe she wouldn't have to conduct a search. She could always hold on to that hope, at least for today.

After removing his hand from beneath her clothes, Raf rimmed the shell of her ear with his tongue. "I have wanted to do that since the first day we rode together. You are very responsive."

"And you are very, very wicked." She laid a hand on his thigh. "I can't reach you to return the favor."

"I will allow that soon enough."

Her phone began its strident ringing, interrupting Imogene's euphoria. She pulled the modern-day demon from her waistband and noted it was her personal burr in the buttocks. "What's wrong now, Sid? You got a hangnail?"

"Real funny, Danforth. Lovell is threatening to take his business elsewhere if he doesn't see you soon. You've got to get back here."

Imogene sighed. Mr. Lovell was one of her best—and wealthiest—clients. She couldn't afford the loss of his business. "Okay. Set up a meeting for tomorrow morning."

"He wants to see you today. What am I supposed to tell him?"

"Be creative, Sid. Tell him I'm sick or out of town. He's a reasonable man. He'll wait twenty-four hours."

"You better hope he does, Danforth. This is your last chance."

She snapped off the phone and shoved it back into the holder attached to her pants. Tomorrow she would have to embark on her return to reality, and she hated that thought.

"You will be leaving soon?" Raf asked in an even tone.

"Looks like it. I've put my boss off as long as I can."

"I thought you were learning to ride per his instructions. Does he not understand what this entails?"

She glanced back at Raf to find him frowning. "Sid only understands the power of money. So I guess this means we're going to have to work very hard today."

"One more day will not be enough."

Imogene would have to agree. Not enough time to learn all she needed to know. Not enough time left with Raf. "I'll have to take my chances, I guess. Or I could come back on Saturday and take up where we left off."

"That would be favorable," Raf said as they entered a break in the woods where a large area leading to the river had been cleared. He stopped near one cypress hanging over the break and dismounted, pulled Imogene from the horse, then secured BáHar's reins on one limb.

She propped her hands on her hips and stared at Raf when he began unbuttoning his shirt. Even though she'd seen his chest several times, she couldn't claim to be impervious to the incredible sight. "Obviously, we're done riding for now."

With his hand poised on his fly, he smiled. "I thought it would be a good day for a swim. Then we will return to the arena for your lesson."

Imogene glanced at the river that looked a little too

muddy for her taste. "I can't imagine what's lurking in there. And the current looks pretty strong."

He shrugged out of his jeans and briefs, leaving him totally nude and extremely proud. All of him. "I will make certain you are not carried away, at least not by the current."

How could she possibly resist him? Easy. She couldn't. With that in mind, she unbuttoned her blouse and slipped it off along with her bra. She had a little more trouble with her boots and had to use a tree trunk for support. By the time she had the pants and underwear off, Raf was already in the water.

He went under for a few moments then rose up like some mythical sea god and slicked his dark hair away from his equally legendary face. His chest glistened in the sun, a solid, rippling mass of male beauty. And Imogene planned to enjoy it to the fullest.

When she started to pick through the debris on the ground to join Raf, her phone rang again.

"Do not answer it," Raf said, his gray eyes narrowed with frustration as he stalked toward the bank.

"I have to see who it is." As if she didn't know. But when she fished the phone out of its holder and depressed the connect button, Raf snatched the cell from her grasp and raised his hand.

Imogene shouted, "Don't you dare!" but not before he hurled it into the river. For a few seconds she could do nothing but stare, her mouth hanging open like a sprung door. "Why did you do that?"

He tugged her into his arms. "I do not want any more interruptions."

"That phone was very expensive."

He burrowed his face in her neck. "I will buy you several before you leave."

Did he have to keep reminding her she was leaving? And

did he have to sound so nonchalant about it? "I'll definitely hold you to that."

He guided her hand down to his erection. "I would prefer you hold this."

She grinned. "What about our swim?"

"I am getting to that."

He picked her up and pulled her legs around his waist, then carried her into the water. He kissed her then, deeply, insistently, while turning them around in a slow circle. Imogene was dizzy from the motion, light-headed from the sheer pleasure of being in his arms.

When he broke the kiss, he slid her down his body until her feet touched the sandy bottom and they were fitted perfectly together. Only one thing would bring them closer.

She pushed his hair back from his face—a face she wouldn't mind waking up to every morning. "This is nice," she said.

"Too often I forget to enjoy the simplicity of nature."

She whisked a kiss along his shadowed jaw. "Me, too. In fact, I spend most of my time indoors, taking care of business."

"I despise the business of running the stable. I would prefer to work with the horses. Before I left Amythra, I spent most of my time training."

"Why don't you hire someone to take care of the business side now?"

"I am very particular. I prefer to handle it myself."

Imogene slid her hand down his belly and below. "Are you sure about that?"

His grin gave the sun a run for its money. "I suppose that does not hold true in every instance."

As promised, Imogene returned the favor, at least for the time Raf allowed it before he said "Enough" and pulled her hand back to his chest.

"You are no fun," Imogene said as she tilted her pelvis against him.

"That is not what you said—"

"I know. Last night."

He feathered kisses along her jaw as he lightly stroked her breast. "I am beginning to believe that clothing is over-rated. Perhaps we should skip that formality for the rest of the day."

"We almost have. But I'm not sure I want to try to ride naked. Besides, what would Ali and Blaylock think?"

He nailed her with a serious stare. "I am the only one entitled to that pleasure."

Imogene decided he might be entitled now, but after she was gone, would he find someone else to replace her? After she returned to Savannah, she would have no control over what he did or with whom he did it. She refused to spoil this heavenly interlude with those concerns.

Just when Raf ran his hands down her bottom and kissed her again, Imogene was suddenly aware of the sound of horse hooves approaching.

"Someone's coming." Her voice came out in a panicked whisper.

"That is my plan."

"I'm serious, Raf."

Raf's gaze snapped to the bank the moment the bay horse and rider came into view. He set Imogene down and pulled her behind him, concealing her from Ali who had stopped near a copse of trees, his gaze averted. "Forgive me for the interruption, Sheikh Shakir, but Ms. Danforth has a call awaiting her at the stables."

"She is occupied at the moment," Raf said. "Tell him she will return the call later."

Ali focused his attention on the sky. "This is not a man. This is Ms. Danforth's mother. She insisted on waiting until I retrieved Ms. Danforth."

Imogene's chest constricted with alarm. "Is it an emergency?"

"She sounded concerned but she did not mention an emergency."

That was welcome news to Imogene. If it had been a crisis, her mother would have said as much. However, with her family's recent problems involving the campaign and sabotage, anything was possible. "Tell her I'll call her as soon as we can get back to the barn."

Ali nodded without looking at her. "I will inform her of that. And again, my apologies." He turned and spurred the horse into a gallop, disappearing in a matter of seconds.

Again Raf pulled Imogene into his arms. "Do you think she could possibly wait awhile longer?"

As much as Imogene wanted to say yes, she couldn't. Her mother wasn't one to overreact so the call had to be important. "We can continue this later in the tub. Right now I need to see what she needs."

"Of course. Your family and your job are more important than our afternoon outing." His tone was flat, emotionless, but Imogene could see the tempest brewing in his eyes right before he dropped his arms and started up the bank without even a parting kiss.

During the journey back to the stable, Raf remained silent and stoic. Imogene couldn't imagine why he was in such a weird mood, but she supposed it was his possessive nature coming out. That might be flattering under some circumstances but she would expect him to understand in this instance. Her family did need her and she intended to be there for them. Her job was an essential part of her life.

Her relationship with Raf was becoming significant, as well. Almost too significant. Imogene had to remember that although they had shared as much as any man and woman could share in terms of intimacy, no promises had been made. No mention of seeing each other beyond the present.

That probably wouldn't happen unless she made the suggestion, something she would have to decide later.

She left Raf in the barn tacking up Maurice for the lesson while she made the call home in the upstairs apartment. She barely got out a greeting before her mother started in.

"Imogene, are you okay?"

"Yes, Mom, I'm fine. What's wrong?"

"My God, I thought you'd been kidnapped. I heard the phone pick up and then you shouted. I was imagining all sorts of things."

Miranda Danforth couldn't begin to imagine what had really been happening between her daughter and the sheikh. "I'm sorry, Mom. Raf kind of took the phone from me and tossed it aside. Sid had just called for about the hundredth time and Raf was getting a little put-out over the interruptions."

"Oh, honey, I didn't mean to interrupt."

"We hadn't really gotten started yet." Darn it. "Did you need something important?"

"Actually, I wanted to remind you of Reid and Tina's wedding on Saturday."

"I remember." In truth, Imogene had forgotten it happened to be this particular weekend.

"We're holding the reception at Crofthaven and I'm overseeing the arrangements. I could use your help."

"Surely Uncle Abraham hired a caterer. After all, it is his son's wedding."

"Of course, but you know how that goes. Someone needs to make certain everything's done correctly. And besides, I've been like a mother to Reid. I want everything to be perfect for him."

In her rational mind, Imogene understood how much this meant to her mother and to Reid, who had lost his own mother in an automobile accident years ago. Since that time, her parents had served as surrogates to Reid and his siblings. In fact, Uncle Abraham's children had been closer to Imogene's parents than their own father, at least until recently.

Imogene couldn't resent her mom and dad for being so loving. And she couldn't let her mother down. "Okay, Mom, I have to come in to work tomorrow, anyway, so I'll be there to help you out."

"You're such a sweetheart for doing this, Imogene. I really appreciate it. I'll see you on Saturday and I'll give you a big hug."

The sincerity in her mother's voice and knowing she had pleased her almost made the chore worthwhile for Imogene. Almost. In her heart she knew that when she returned to Savannah, she wouldn't have the opportunity to come back to the stables, or to Raf, at least not for a while.

She sensed Raf would require more of her time than she had to give if they decided to pursue their relationship beyond this weekend. To do anything less would be unfair to him. Of course, he hadn't even hinted at that, so she had nothing to worry about at all. Except for the fact that she was totally, unequivocally in love with him.

"Is she the one, Rafi?"

Raf paused with his hand on the saddle's girth strap, shocked by Ali's query. He opted for ignorance instead of providing an answer. "I assume you are referring to the filly. I believe she will serve as evidence of BáHar's abilities to reproduce."

"I am referring to Ms. Danforth, as you well know. Is she a diversion, or is she quite possibly the woman you have chosen to save you from this meaningless existence you have made for yourself?"

"I do not understand why you have assumed such a thing."

"I've suspected for some time now that you and Ms.

Danforth are not simply teacher and student. What I witnessed earlier has confirmed that fact.''

Raf cinched the saddle tightly, then loosened it somewhat for Maurice's sake. ''I trust that what you witnessed earlier will go no further than this conversation.''

''You know you do not have to question my loyalty. And you have yet to answer my question. Will she be staying longer than first assumed?''

''Ms. Danforth will be leaving tomorrow and will return on Saturday. Beyond that, we have no immediate plans for the future. And that is the end of this conversation.''

Raf dropped the bridle twice while trying to slip it into Maurice's mouth. He muttered an oath under his breath.

''Do you wish me to assist you, Rafi?''

Raf looked up to see Ali still scrutinizing him. ''I do not require your assistance. I could do this in my sleep.''

Ali rubbed his bearded chin, a smile playing at the corners of his mouth. ''I fear that is what you are trying to do now. Did you not sleep last night?''

Raf did not appreciate his friend's continued prodding. ''I am rested. Thank you for your concern.''

Ali leaned back against the stall, arms folded across his chest, looking very much like a stern father. ''Will you have Ms. Danforth canter today?''

Raf cinched the saddle's girth. ''Not yet. She is not quite ready.''

''Are you certain? Since she has such a short while before she departs, I would think you might wish to accelerate her lessons.''

''I will determine when she will move to the next step.''

''Are you being overly cautious because of past experience? Or are you attempting to prolong her time here?''

Normally Raf would not resent Ali's queries. After all, the man was a good friend. Yet today he did not have the patience nor did he want to be reminded of past failures.

"I would prefer to err on the side of caution, and I do not wish to discuss the matter further."

"You care greatly for her," Ali stated. "More than you are willing to acknowledge."

Raf turned from the gelding and leveled his gaze on Ali, who seemed determined not to give up. "You are imagining things, old man."

"I am not so old that I cannot recognize when a man is completely enchanted with a woman. And you are, my friend."

"Believe what you will."

Ali approached Raf and laid a hand on his shoulder. "When your father lost your mother, he did not stop living. He would not be pleased to know that you have chosen that path."

Raf shook off his hand. "Look around you. I am living quite well."

"Yet you have no one to share in your life."

"My father did not see the need to do that after my mother's death."

"He had you and Darin, and he also had a long-time mistress, the same lover until his death."

"I am aware of that, but I do not understand the point of this conversation, unless you are saying I should have Ms. Danforth as my mistress."

"I am not saying that. She deserves to be more than your mistress."

Raf remained silent, fearing that if he said anything else, he would surely give his feelings for Genie away. As much as he wanted to believe that Genie could become a permanent part of his life, he could not trust that she would want the same. That she would have room for him in her life. He would not want to interfere in her goals, and should he decide to commit to a woman, he did not want to be an afterthought. A diversion.

"As I have said repeatedly, I have no intention of becoming seriously involved with anyone at present." He sounded more convinced than he felt.

When Ali cleared his throat and nodded, Raf looked to his left to see Genie standing in the aisle not more than a few feet away. He had no idea how much of the conversation she had heard although she did not appear to be distressed. Perhaps she was even relieved to know he did not view their liaison as a permanent relationship. At least that was the impression he'd wanted to give. In truth, he wanted much more from her.

Ali took his leave when Genie approached and gave Maurice a pat on his neck. "Are we ready for the lesson?"

"We are," Raf said. "Was your mother well?"

"Sure. She needed to remind me of my cousin's wedding Saturday. I promised to help her with the reception."

Disappointment weighed heavily on Raf's heart, but he covered it with an cool expression. "Then you will not be returning on Saturday?"

"I won't have time."

"And the week after?"

She looked away. "I have to go back to work, so I guess we'd better get to work on my riding skills." She brought her attention to him again. "I'm ready for the next step."

"You cannot learn how to canter in one lesson."

"I'll just have to do the best that I can. Maybe I can come back a couple of times to practice before I have to impress the Granthams."

"If that is what you wish, but I cannot promise you will be ready."

"I'm not asking for any promises from you."

A lengthy silence ensued before Raf finally said, "Then we are agreed. No promises." That sealed his beliefs about his relationship with Genie and where it would not lead. She wanted nothing more than his expertise. Their time together had been nothing more than a means to pass the time. Her life could not include a lengthy relationship with him.

With Genie hanging back a few steps, he led Maurice into the arena where Ali waited, as he'd requested the last few lessons. Although he did not need his friend's attendance, he felt it wise to have him there, to correct any mistakes Genie might make due to Raf's continued lack of concentration in her presence.

All three entered the arena, and Genie mounted the gelding without Raf's help. He had to acknowledge that she had come a long way in a very short time. But was she ready to canter?

"Perhaps I should utilize the *longe* line," he told Ali.

"She will manage alone. I have already shown her how to cue the correct lead and how to sit the horse."

"When?"

"In your absence. She is prepared for this."

Raf summoned his resolve to keep his temper in check. Again he felt as if he had been cast off regarding her instruction. Yet he had to recognize that Ali was an expert rider and teacher. That still did nothing to quell Raf's displeasure, or his guardedness where Genie's safety was concerned. It would not be beneficial for her if she sensed his wariness.

For that reason he told Ali, "I will allow you to take it from here."

Ali's dark brows drew down. "Are you certain?"

"Yes. I will stand by the gate to observe."

Before Ali could protest, Raf strode to the far side of the arena near the gate to watch as Ali instructed Genie to walk, then trot, and finally, to canter, while Raf sent up a silent prayer for her safety.

Raf was amazed at how easily she had taken the gait, how well she sat the horse as Maurice cantered around the arena. Her pride came out in a smile as she passed by him—a smile that Raf would long remember, even after she left him for good.

Genie made the rounds twice more with confidence, proving to Raf he had been wrong about her skills. She was a natural—at riding and at lovemaking. His concerns began to drift away as he took in the beauty of the sight…until the unthinkable happened.

A strong wind tossed around dirt and debris in the arena, bringing with it a plastic sack that landed in the path of horse and rider. Maurice, who rarely balked at anything, chose that moment to forget his training and rear up, tossing Genie to one side. She tried to right herself but to no avail. In a tangle of limbs, clawing the air on her descent, she fell into a cloud of dust.

And Raf Shakir faced his past, his greatest fear, once more.

Nine

A perfect three-point landing on her butt.

Imogene tested all her limbs. No damage done, as far as she could tell. She dusted off the front of her blouse and pants, but unfortunately she couldn't remove the dust from her nose, the reason why she sneezed several times. She wiped her teary eyes with the back of her hand, clearing her vision enough to see Raf crouched beside her, his eyes reflecting concern and something that looked a great deal like fear.

"Are you injured?" he asked.

She attempted a weak smile despite her momentary alarm. "I'm okay. Just a little rattled. It happened so fast I couldn't quite right myself. I tried."

Ali returned her smile when Raf didn't. "You recovered well."

Raf eyed her with suspicion. "Are you certain you are not in pain?"

"Nothing's hurt, except maybe my pride." And her feelings over his harsh tone.

"Regardless, I should call a doctor," Raf said.

"That's not necessary." She hopped to her feet and swiped her hands over her bottom in order to prove to Raf she was A-okay. He didn't seem at all pleased by that when he straightened, his hands fisted at his sides.

Imogene scanned the arena to find the gelding trying to stick his head through the fencing to pilfer a few random pieces of grass. "Looks like Maurice is none the worse for wear."

"He is fine," Ali said. "I am surprised the bag caused him to bolt. Normally he is very steady."

Imogene wiped her hands on her thighs. "Guess you can't blame him. I doubt he's ever been shopping in a superstore before."

Ali's grin deepened. "Perhaps I should hang a few bags in his stall so that he will grow accustomed to them."

"I'm sure that will be fine with him, as long as you fill them with candy."

Imogene and Ali shared a laugh while Raf stood silently by, his lips forming a grim line. "I believe you have had enough for the day," he said, his tone again severe, as if he blamed her for the little mishap.

"I want to get back on him and try again," she said.

Raf's eyes narrowed with anger. "Impossible."

Imogene decided to stand her ground now that it was firmly planted beneath her feet. "No, it's not. I might not know much about horses, but I do know you're supposed to get back on after a fall. Right, Ali?"

Although Ali looked uncomfortable, he nodded. "That is correct."

Raf glared at Ali, then at Imogene. "I do not want to be responsible for any injury that might occur. As I have said, you are not ready."

She braced her hands on her hips, "I'm more than ready, and you know it. And I'm not going to hold you responsible. I'm a big girl and I make my own decisions."

"I will not be a party to it."

"You don't have to. Ali can stay while I make a few more rounds."

Raf's gaze snapped to Ali. "He will not agree."

Ali rubbed a hand over his bearded chin. "Ms. Danforth is aware of the risk, as are you, Rafi. She should continue the lesson."

Without another word, Raf turned away and stormed out of the arena, mounted BáHar and took off at a run toward the river. Imogene would allow him time to cool off before she had her say. Later she would attempt to make him understand that although she appreciated his concern for her, it was unwarranted. She could master this whole riding thing, and in the process she would make him proud, whether he admitted it or not.

Imogene readjusted the chin strap on the black velvet hard hat. "Thanks for doing this, Ali. I hope this doesn't get you into too much trouble."

"I am not concerned about the repercussions of assisting you. Once he has some time to think, he will recognize that we have done the right thing."

"I don't understand why he was so upset. Surely he's had other students who've taken a tumble. In fact, he's probably taken a few himself."

"That is true, but he is recalling one particular student."

As Imogene had suspected, Raf's caution was personal. "A student who got hurt during the course of a lesson?"

"Not only a student. His wife."

Just as Imogene's pulse had begun to return to normal, it shot to life again over the revelation. "His wife was hurt?"

"While Sheikh Shakir looked on."

Imogene was suddenly aware that all her questions about Raf could soon be answered. Even more aware that the severity of his turmoil might be greater than she'd ever envisioned. "Oh, God. How bad was it?"

Ali again looked somewhat disconcerted. "What I tell you now might be deemed a lapse in loyalty to a man whom I consider a friend. Yet I tell you out of concern for Rafi and so that you will understand his behavior."

The lesson forgotten, Imogene followed Ali to the edge of the arena, leaned against the fencing and prepared to learn what she'd longed to know for days. But she couldn't have been prepared for what Ali told her.

His calm tone belied the tumult that had been Raf Shakir's past—a man who had married a young woman for only a brief time before an equestrian accident had claimed her life. Although Ali did not give much information beyond that, Imogene didn't require the gritty details to know that Raf had suffered a tremendous loss and an overriding guilt because he'd believed he was at fault. He still suffered from that guilt and loss.

And to think Imogene had believed his wife had left him, or vice versa. How could she not have known his problems ran so much deeper than that? And why had everyone been so evasive with those details, especially Doris? Plain and simple, they had been trying to protect him. But Imogene knew all too well that no matter how cautious a person might be, protecting a loved one from misfortune wasn't always possible.

In that moment, when she finally understood the trouble that followed Raf, the realization that she, too, had buried herself in her own guilt hit home. She couldn't have protected Tori from everything, and Raf couldn't have foreseen what would happen to his wife after he'd been so diligent in his teaching. Despite their differences, in many ways she and Raf were the same.

She would climb back on the horse, finish her lesson and regain her confidence. But she didn't feel at all confident over the confrontation she would soon have with Raf. She didn't know what she would say to him. She did know that she couldn't leave here tomorrow until she made things right between them, even if the possibility of making things work had shattered when she'd learned that quite possibly she had been merely a replacement for a woman he still loved. As much as Imogene cared for him, she could never accept that role.

All for the best, she supposed. Her life was too demanding. She had too much to do, too many places to see, a career to build. Then why did she feel as if none of that really mattered anymore?

Because it was beginning not to matter. Her feelings for Raf had clouded her judgment and confused her. Still, he loved someone else, so the point was moot.

They did have this one last night together, and she would carry that with her always—if she could convince Raf to cooperate. She wanted to spend the night making love with him, and she planned to do that very thing, but this time on her terms.

As Raf returned to the stable with BáHar, the wind had quieted somewhat but his turmoil had not. Seeing Genie fall from the horse had been the equivalent of a recurring nightmare. Even though she had been unharmed, even though he had purposely been overly cautious, he still felt responsible for the accident. He had not been able to shelter her from the fall no matter how greatly he had wanted to do that very thing. He also had not been able to prevent falling in love with her.

That realization had been as difficult to accept as knowing he'd failed to protect her. Looking back on his life, he now understood that he had never been in love with a woman before, and he was not certain what to do with the information he now held.

If he spoke of his feelings for her, he would most likely face certain rejection. Tomorrow she was leaving. As he'd known from the beginning, she was committed solely to her career and her family. He had no place in her life, even if she would always occupy a place in his heart.

After settling BáHar for the night, Raf walked down the aisle toward his office, only to be met by Ali. "I have taken care of the stallion," he told him as he continued past him. "I will see you in the morning."

"Do you not wish to know how Ms. Danforth did during the lesson?" Ali asked.

Raf slowed his steps but did not face his friend. "I'm certain she did well and you no doubt are determined to stress that point."

"Yes, she did well. And I have a question for you before you retire."

Although he wanted to keep going, Raf turned out of respect. "I hope this is important. I have some business to attend to before I go to bed."

"When will you stop running, my friend?"

Anger again surfaced from the place Raf had purposely kept concealed. "I am not running from anything or anyone. I need time alone to think."

"Does this involve your decision about your relationship with Ms. Danforth?"

"There is nothing to decide."

"Then you will not ask her to stay?"

Raf had considered that, but he could not bear to hear her refusal. "She has no reason to stay. She has a life beyond this stable."

"And you have no life beyond this place. You do have the opportunity to alter that fate."

"My relationship with Ms. Danforth…" Raf clenched his teeth and spoke through them. *"Háadha mub zayn."*

"Not good?" Ali smiled. "My friend, this is too good with Ms. Danforth, and that is why you choose to run."

Clinging to the last thread of restraint, Raf said, with as much calm as he could gather, "We have discussed this before, Ali. I have no desire to enter into a permanent relationship with a woman who would rather be somewhere else. I will not make that mistake again."

Ali stood silently for a moment, but Raf could tell he was not finished with his unwelcome advice. "Letting her go without finding out how she feels will be the most crucial mistake you could make. Think long and hard about that, Rafi. Otherwise, you will live with more regrets."

Raf turned and escaped to the apartment before he had to endure more of Ali's commentary on the unfortunate state of his life. After settling behind his desk, he mulled over his friend's words. No matter how much he longed to be with Genie, it would be best to end their relationship tomorrow morning. He would not burden her with his feelings or force her to decide between him and her freedom. That would be his gift to her in return for all that she had given him.

He had to come to bed at some point in time.

At least Imogene wanted to believe that as she waited in his suite after climbing from her own lonely bed a few minutes before to seek him out. She'd never been in his room before, one of the *only* places they hadn't made love, and she was surprised by the suite's starkness. The furniture was solid pine, square, the spread a plain navy blue. No keepsakes, no frills, no pictures of his former wife. That might have shocked her if she hadn't known him better. He wouldn't want any obvious reminders; he had enough of those stored in his memory.

Now well past midnight, she decided she might as well give up and go to bed—alone. After all, she had to be up in order to allow enough travel time for her return to Savannah for her meeting. She would have to stop by the condo first to dress in her work clothes. She would need at least an hour to cry.

Funny, she hadn't cried in a long time, and she couldn't imagine why she felt the need now. She'd had limited experience with significant goodbyes, the most recent being her parting with Wayne. But she hadn't felt as deeply for him as she did for Raf. She hadn't given all of herself, heart and soul, to Wayne the way she had with Raf. She hadn't sighed when he'd made love to her, hadn't craved him so desperately that she physically ached at the thought of not seeing him for even a day. She hadn't shed any tears over him.

No denying it, she'd spent most of her adulthood avoiding situations that led to goodbyes, but she couldn't avoid this one—the mother of them all. And she wasn't going to allow Raf to avoid her on their final night together. If he ever returned to his room.

The opening door startled Imogene, sending her from the chair she'd been occupying next to his bed. He halted when he caught sight of her, his hand still on the knob as if he might try to escape. Not if Imogene could help it.

She lifted her chin, displaying a bravado she didn't feel in the least. "I was wondering when you might finally turn in. Where've you been?"

He dropped his hand from the door but left it open. "In the downstairs library. I could not sleep so I did some reading."

"I couldn't sleep, either."

Now what? Imogene thought when the only thing that seemed to exist between them was silence. Seeing him dressed in a gaping robe and pajamas made her want to skip the conversation and just kiss him. But he looked so guarded, her own insecurity kept her in place. "Since I'm leaving tomorrow morning, I thought we might spend some time together."

"I would not be good company."

"You're always good company, Raf."

"That could be debated after today." He sounded somewhat contrite and weary.

Imogene convened all her courage, knowing she was taking a risk by bringing up what she'd learned from Ali. But she didn't want to leave with so much unsaid, without him knowing how well she knew his grief. "Why didn't you tell me about your wife's death?"

He didn't even try to hide his anger. "Who informed you of her death?"

"Ali. But don't be too hard on him. He did it out of concern for you. I just wish you had told me first."

"I did not want to be forced to explain."

"Why? Did you really think I wouldn't understand?"

He looked away. "The past should remain in the past."

She took his hands into hers and gave them a gentle squeeze. "It should, but it has a way of rearing its head whether we want it to or not."

"I am not in the mood to talk about this." His tone was stern, but at least he didn't pull away.

She slipped her arms around his waist and settled her cheek against his heart. "We don't have to talk at all."

After a few minutes she raised her gaze to his. "Tonight I don't want to think about the past or the future. I just want to be with you."

Imogene saw a glimmer of hesitation in his dark eyes before he sighed and bracketed her face in his palms. "Why do I find it so difficult to deny you?"

She rested her hand on his. "Because you know how good we've been together, and it will be good between us again. However, you might change your mind when I tell you my requests.''

Finally, he smiled—a soft smile that held a world of emotion. ''Would these requests involve the mirror?''

She took his hands and pulled him down onto the edge of his bed. ''Not tonight. No mirrors, just us.''

''Then we will have no mirrors.''

''And I don't want you to close your eyes, not even for a minute. I want you to see me, Raf. Make love to *me*.''

He framed her face in his palms and tipped his forehead against her. ''I will do anything you ask, Genie. Anything.''

She knew he would when it came to her physical pleasure, but he wasn't capable of giving her the one thing she needed most—his love, at least not until he dealt with his own demons. That might never happen. Regardless, she would love him tonight with all she had to give.

They stood by the bed and undressed each other in the glow of the bedside lamp that allowed them to visually explore without any reticence. Although they had done this many times in the past two weeks, these moments were so very special, at least to Imogene. Most likely the final moments they would share in this familiarity.

Once more they held each other before Raf took her down onto the bed in his arms and kissed her. A deep, meaningful kiss that conveyed their desire for each other, their absolute need.

Raf held nothing back when he loved Imogene, using his hands and lips with tender persuasion over the territory he now knew so well. Imogene submitted to his skill, watching while he brought her to a shattering climax with his mouth. She explored the length of his body with her mouth and hands, as well, taking him to the brink before he pulled her up into his arms.

Keeping his eyes fixed on hers, Raf eased into her then lifted her arms above her head to entwine their fingers.

Such sweet torture, Imogene thought as Raf moved inside of her. Such sweet, sweet surrender.

"This is too good," he said, his gaze firmly locked with hers.

"It can never be too good," she told him.

"I want it to last," he said. "It *has* to last."

Imogene wanted it to last, too—forever. That wasn't reality, but Raf was real. His touch was so real. And her love for him was infinitely real.

As always, he found ways to bring her to another climax, using his hands and body until she was completely absorbed in the heady sensations. Soon after, Raf's jaw went taut and Imogene witnessed the moment he climaxed while looking into his dark, soulful eyes. A word she didn't understand hissed from his lips before he collapsed against her. She held him tightly as he trembled in her arms. They seemed suspended in time for endless, magical moments, and that was okay with Imogene. As far as she was concerned, they could go on this way forever.

Raf finally moved away from Imogene and snapped off the bedside lamp, the room now illuminated only by the guard light filtering in from the windows. He stretched out on his back and slid his arm beneath her, bringing her to rest against his chest as he lazily brushed his fingertips down her arm.

Shadows played along the walls and over his distinctive profile. He'd closed his eyes, and Imogene wondered what he was thinking, or about whom. Was he remembering his wife and what they'd shared? Was he regretting it was Imogene, not her, in his arms?

She would never know because she didn't want to know. She'd rather go back home believing that the lovemaking they'd shared in these midnight hours was all about them, not someone who'd once been in his life.

Imogene heard the low rumble of thunder then the steady

sound of raindrops against the windows that seemed to keep time with Raf's strong heart beating against her cheek. She thought it somewhat ironic that they'd come full circle, making love the first and last time in the presence of a deluge. Fitting, considering she suspected Raf still had a storm brewing inside him. And so did she.

Turning onto her side, away from Raf, she bit the inside of her mouth to keep from sobbing, especially when he fitted himself to her back, one arm draped over her hip. And here they were, spooning like ordinary lovers, yet there was nothing ordinary about the prince. Beneath the serious, regal demeanor, a strong, loving man existed—a man who possessed a wounded heart that Imogene couldn't heal.

She refused to waste precious moments worrying about things she couldn't control. Right now she only wanted to take pleasure in him holding her close, catalogue the memories to bring out on another stormy day.

After a time, the rain falling in a lullaby rhythm lulled Imogene into drowsiness. Although she didn't want to fritter away the rest of the night, she could no longer fight the lure of sleep.

For the first time in years, as Imogene Danforth drifted off, her final thoughts did not involve guilt over her sister's disappearance. They centered solely on her love for Sheikh Raf Shakir.

As Raf held Genie in the hours before dawn, he vowed he would give her whatever her heart desired—if she asked it of him. Yet he had known from the beginning that she would ask nothing of him, the reason why he had not hesitated to become involved with her. Now he longed for her to want something from him aside from physical pleasure, anything, even his love. That love for her had flourished each time they had been together, no matter where they had been—in the arena while he'd watched her perfect her riding skills, or in the midst of sleep as he watched her now.

Yet if he could not have her for all time, he could have her once more before morning arrived, taking her from him for good.

On that thought, he pressed against her back as he slid the sheet down her arm and over the bow of her hip, uncovering her curves for his hands. When he reached her thigh, he diverted his path to the warmth between her legs, touching her lightly yet insistently. He knew the moment she came awake when she reached back and ran her hand over his buttocks then lifted his leg over her hip. He did not have to ask what she wanted. They had become so attuned to each other's desires, words were not necessary.

He stopped touching her only long enough to guide himself inside her, uniting them once more. While caressing her with his fingertips, he tried with all his might to temper his thrusts, to no avail. She encouraged him with her soft sounds of pleasure until control was no longer an option.

They moved together in a reckless, primal rhythm as all thoughts of the past or future gave way to the present when nothing mattered aside from this perfect joining. Genie climaxed first, drawing Raf farther into her body until he relinquished his resistance, giving in to his body's demand for release with a jolt that had him shaking from its force.

When his body calmed, he turned Genie over and sought her mouth, taking to memory each nuance of her taste, the texture of her tongue, though he knew he would not soon forget.

He pulled away and met her heavy-lidded gaze. "Please tell me it's not morning," she said.

He kissed her lips again, softly. "Not yet, but soon."

She closed her eyes and covered her mouth with her hand to conceal a yawn. "Good. I'm not ready to get up yet."

Raf was not ready for her to go and he said as much when he murmured, *"La trúuH."*

Her eyes snapped open. "What did you say?"

He could not ask her to stay so that she could understand, not without facing her certain refusal. "I said you should go back to sleep." The lie tasted bitter going down.

He settled her back into his arms and stroked her hair until he felt her body grow slack against his, her breathing now slow and steady.

He cursed his own cowardice, his inability to express his emotions because of his fears. If only he knew of some way to convince her to stay. Considering her devotion to her job and family, he doubted anything he might say would be convincing enough...unless.

Raf allowed a smile to form when he remembered that Genie prided herself on being a negotiator. Well, so was he. Perhaps that would be the only way to reach her.

"You want me to do what?"

"Come to work for me."

Imogene stood with her hand frozen on her car door. "Doing what?"

"Running the business while I work with the horses. It should prove to be challenging enough for you."

Earlier that morning after they'd showered together, he'd said he had something he wanted to ask her before she left, then he'd kept her in suspense all through breakfast. Of course, Imogene had been naive enough to assume he'd meant something a little more romantic. Not a marriage proposal, but at least that he wanted to see her again. How stupid she'd been to think such a thing. "I have a job, but thanks for the offer." And she had a heartache the size of his house.

He rested one arm on the top of her car and assumed a confident and almost insolent posture. "I will allow you time to consider it. Call me when you've reached your decision.''

''I've already decided, Raf. No thanks. I have big plans.'' The first being she was going to bawl like a baby when she left him.

After she checked her watch to avoid his compelling eyes, she said, ''I really have to go now.''

When she opened the car door, he pushed it closed with his palm. ''We have not discussed when and where I am to deliver BáHar to your clients' farm.''

Imogene's thought he'd made a mistake. ''BáHar?''

''Of course. You've said you wanted a good mount to impress your clients, and you must admit he is quite impressive.''

''But you've said that no one is allowed—''

''To touch him, I know.'' He reached out and tucked her hair behind her ear, a familiar gesture Imogene had come to appreciate. ''I believe in you, Genie. I know you will not disappoint your clients, or me.''

A baseball-size lump formed in her throat. ''You really have that much faith in me?''

He pulled her hand from the door and brought it to his lips. ''Yes, I do. You have shown me your skills.'' And he showed her his wicked side with a smile that made her want to melt into the pavement. ''You have convinced me of your expertise. And that is why I trust you to run my business.''

Oh, how she wanted to scrap her responsibility and say yes. But she had to be strong and not prolong the agony any longer than necessary. She didn't want to work with him; she wanted to love him, and for him to love her back.

Imogene tugged her hand from his grasp and again opened the door. This time he didn't stop her. ''Actually, I'm going to tell the Granthams the truth, that I have very little experience with horses and that I don't own one. I've decided honesty is really the best policy in this instance. If they aren't impressed by my business acumen, then I don't want their business.''

''Are you certain?''

''Yes.''

''Then you have wasted your time here.''

Raf's solemn tone, his words, caused Imogene's heart to clutch painfully in her chest. ''Believe me, I don't consider the past two weeks a waste at all. I've learned a lot about who I am and what I want.''

He rested his palms on her shoulders and studied her with sincerity, with some unknown emotion reflecting from his eyes. ''What do you want, Genie?''

You. ''I want to work hard and be the best I can be at whatever I do. I also plan to forgive myself for what happened to my sister. I realize I had no control over what happened to her, even if I still hold out hope we'll find her. In a way, you've taught me that.'' She sighed. ''Now I have a favor to ask of you.''

''What would that be?''

She cupped his jaw in her palm. ''I want you to forgive yourself, too. You couldn't have prevented what happened to your wife. I want you to be happy.''

Raf drew her into an embrace and held her closely. When he pulled away, he looked as if he wanted to say something more. Instead he stepped back and held open the car door. ''Be safe, Genie. Call me if you change your mind about my offer.''

So that's it, Imogene thought as she climbed into the car and he closed the door. But she didn't intend to drive away until she had one last thing from him. After rolling down the window, she said, ''Kiss me goodbye, Sheikh Shakir.''

He leaned over and kissed her so completely she considered getting out of the car and baring her soul. After he was done creating enough heat in her to incinerate the sedan, she turned the ignition and he turned away without saying goodbye.

That was okay with Imogene. Though she knew this goodbye could be for good, she at least didn't have to hear the ugly word. Yet as she steered the car down the road, glancing at the house in the rearview mirror to find Raf standing on the porch, watching her leave, she could almost hear him say it. And she immediately regretted what she hadn't said, that she loved him.

Regardless that they couldn't be together permanently, Imogene had to credit him with the sense of liberation she had experienced in his arms. And that liberation had her questioning her own life and what she really wanted for her future. She had changed over the past two weeks, that much she knew. A change that had been a long time coming. Now she just had to decide what other changes were necessary.

Ten

"**W**hat in the hell do you think you're doing, Danforth?"

Imogene looked up from where she'd been doodling Raf's name on a notepad to find Sid in her office door, looking as if he could blow his cheap toupee right through the office roof. "Nice to see you, too, Sid."

His ruddy face reddened once more with fury. "I just got a call from Pierce Grantham. He said you told him that the whole riding thing was a ruse."

She tossed aside the pencil and watched it roll off the edge of the desk. "That's right, Sid. I told them the truth. And you know what? They didn't seem at all angry."

"Not at you, but they sure as hell are with me. Did you have to tell them this was all my idea?"

"Actually, I didn't say that at all. It seems Mr. Grantham figured that one out on his own."

Sid balled his fists and glared at her. "You've done it now, Danforth. You're...you're..."

"Fired?" Imogene slapped her palms on her desk and stood. "You can't fire me, Sid, because I quit. I've already turned in my resignation to your father-in-law, along with my reasons."

"You can't do that!"

Imogene yanked her jacket from the back of her chair and slipped it on. "I just did. I can deal with the hours, the lack of sleep, but I can't deal with the deception."

She walked out the door without a backward glance, experiencing a surprising sense of freedom for someone who was now unemployed. Of course, she did have one job prospect.

No way. She refused to work for Raf if that's the only role he intended she play in his life. Okay, maybe he did expect them to take up where they'd left off, but she couldn't do that without any form of commitment from him.

Boy, she had changed. A few weeks ago, any kind of commitment beyond her family and job had been out of the question, at least where a relationship with a man was concerned. But that's exactly what she wanted now, some sort of commitment from Raf. Not that she would ever get one—at least, not until he managed to get over the blinding grief and guilt he'd kept bottled up inside.

Imogene refused to be a substitute; she wanted to be the real thing. And until he decided—if he decided—that's what he wanted from her, she would lay low and wait. She could be in for a long, long wait.

The following day Raf sat at the dining room table in the kitchen, leaving his food untouched. He had no use for nourishment at the moment, nor did he have any use for the company he now kept. Doris, Blaylock and Ali were staring at him as if they expected him to make an excuse for his continued silence and his lack of appetite.

He pushed the bowl away and wrapped his hands around the coffee mug, hoping they would leave him with his remorse.

Instead, Doris leaned forward and pinned him with a glare.

"Is she coming back?"

Raf averted his gaze to the financial section of the paper and pretended to peruse the market report. "No."

"And you just let her leave?"

Doris's incredulous tone brought Raf's attention back to her. "I had no say in the matter. Her career imposes demands on her time. She had no reason to stay."

"Oh, good grief," Doris muttered. "Didn't you give her a reason?"

"I made her an offer that she refused."

"She wouldn't marry you?"

"Doris," Blaylock said in a warning tone. "That's none of your business."

Doris waved a dismissive hand in her husband's direction. "Come on, Bernie. Someone needs to tend to his business before he makes the biggest mistake of his life."

"Precisely," Ali said. "I have told him much the same."

Anger rose to the surface of Raf's calm demeanor, threatening to explode in a litany of oaths. He felt as if he sat before a jury who had found him guilty before he'd stated his case. "I did not ask Ms. Danforth to marry me. I asked her to work for me."

Doris rolled her eyes to the ceiling. "All that highfalutin European education and you never learned how to romance a woman." She pointed toward the door. "Bernie, you and Ali go outside and work while I give the sheikh a quick lesson on how to woo a woman."

Blaylock rubbed the back of his neck, looking decidedly uncomfortable. "Doris, I don't think the sheikh—"

This time Raf waved off Blaylock's protests. "Let her speak her mind. She will do as much, anyway."

As soon as Ali and Blaylock left, Doris folded her arms beneath her ample breasts and sat back in the chair. "Now, what are you going to do about getting her back?"

"If she wants to return, she will do so without my coercion."

"I'm not saying you should drag her back here in shackles. You have to convince her with words and actions. Let her know what you're feeling inside."

Raf recognized he should have done that last night or, at the very least, before she'd left him this morning. "I'm afraid I squandered that chance. Therefore, I must wait to see if she returns of her own free will."

"Dammit, man, you don't have time to wait. Go get her."

"I have no idea where to find her." A weak excuse since he had the resources to locate anyone. But he was not certain she wanted to be found. After all, she had not bothered to leave her address or phone number. And he had not bothered to ask.

Doris took the society section of the newspaper, turned it in his direction and pointed at the front-page article. "There's a wedding reception at her uncle's mansion for her cousin tonight. She'll be there."

Raf recalled Imogene mentioning the reception, the reason why she had decided not to return today for a final lesson. "I have not been invited."

"Do you really think they'll kick you out if you don't have an invitation? You just dress up in your royal clothes, tell them you know Miss Imogene, flash them a few bucks and they'll let you in."

Raf could not suppress his smile over Doris's serious expression. "And after I gain entry, what then?"

She blew out a frustrated sigh. "Am I gonna have to tell

you everything? You find her and you tell her you want her to come back, permanently. Unless you don't love her, but I highly doubt that. It's written all over your face."

Raf streaked one hand over his jaw and considered lying, yet he knew Doris would see right through his pretense. "Are my feelings that obvious?"

"Maybe not to some, but I'm a woman, and women know these things. And she's in love with you, too."

Raf did well to hide his shock. "Did she say as much to you?"

"For goodness' sake, she didn't have to say it. I could see it every time she looked at you. Every time you looked at each other. I have never known two more stubborn, foolhardy people. It's time you both get rid of your pride and lay it on the line."

"And what shall I do if she refuses then?"

Taking Raf by surprise, Doris laid a palm on his hand. "She won't refuse you. And if she does, then I'll have a long talk with her, too."

Until that moment Raf hadn't realized how much he had missed not having a woman's counsel in his adulthood. His own mother had died giving birth to his brother, so he had not known any true maternal care aside from a succession of governesses. He appreciated Doris more than he could express, and the least he could do was follow her advice. He would also pray that she was right about Genie's feelings for him.

He would never know unless he asked.

At the wedding reception for her cousin Reid and his new wife, Tina, Imogene sat alone in Crofthaven's ornate ballroom, aimlessly perusing the notable guests. Many attendees she recognized, others she did not and even when the former president had made a brief appearance with secret service agents in tow, she couldn't muster much enthusiasm or excitement.

No one really seemed to notice that she'd been sitting all alone at the lace-covered corner table, holding a full champagne flute while she felt completely empty. The bride and groom didn't seem to notice anyone but each other. Her cousin Kimberly, her one-time best friend, had only spoken to her briefly before joining her new husband, Zachary Sheridan, on the dance floor. Even her own mother and father had spent most of the evening schmoozing, when they weren't clinging to each other like grapevines during their favorite waltzes.

Imogene despised her envy but it seemed the whole world was in love. So was she, the difference being the one she loved was absent from her life, even if not from her thoughts. She'd been tempted to call him up this afternoon and tell him she'd quit her job and that she might consider his offer. But she wanted so much more from him. She still did. She couldn't settle for less.

A sigh slipped from her lips as she rimmed the champagne flute with one neatly painted red nail that matched her red chiffon gown. Her mother hadn't been too pleased that she'd chosen to wear such a vibrant color for the wedding festivities, but she'd done so with Raf in mind since he'd told her several times he preferred her in red. And that was silly considering he would never see the dress.

The tap on her shoulder startled Imogene and she looked back to see her brother's familiar, endearing face. Toby, handsome as ever yet so serious and brooding at times.

"Can I join your little pity party?" he asked.

She pulled out the chair next to her. "Be my guest, but I'm not having a pity party."

Toby sat and scooted the chair beneath the table. "Are you sure? You look like you've lost your best friend."

In many ways Imogene had. "I'm just tired. I've had a rough couple of days." And two very long, lonely nights.

"Mom tells me you've been taking riding lessons at some stable around here. You could've called me. I would've taught you."

"No way, Toby. First, I didn't have time to trek all the way to Wyoming. Second, you and I get along fine as long as you're not trying to tell me what to do. Third, you have your hands full with your child." She looked around and noticed her nephew's absence. "Where is Dylan, anyway?"

"The housekeeper put him to bed. He's not that comfortable with crowds."

"Is he making any progress as far as his speech is concerned?"

"He's still not talking. I keep thinking he will someday, if I'm patient with him. But sometimes I wonder if I'm doing the right thing."

Imogene's heart went out to her brother, who had given his life to raising his three-year-old musically gifted child who had not spoken since his mother's departure. "You're a great dad, Toby. Dylan's lucky to have you."

"I try, but a lot of people believe he needs a mother."

"He doesn't need *his* mother, or at least she obviously doesn't need him. After all, she was the one who abandoned him."

Toby averted his gaze to the dance floor without responding. Imogene assumed he was avoiding any mention of his social-climbing ex-wife who'd had no use for a rancher. Since her departure, Sheila had taken up with some playboy on the Riviera. Good riddance, as far as Imogene and the rest of the family were concerned. But she worried that Toby would never get over those wounds, much the same as Raf.

Raf. How many times had she thought about him today? Too many times to count.

After a span of silence, Toby turned his brotherly concern on Imogene. "What's bugging you, Genie?"

She shrugged. "This atmosphere's getting to me, I guess. I haven't seen Uncle Abraham for about half an hour, so I guess it's getting to him, too, and he's the one who should be mingling for the sake of his campaign."

Toby glanced over his shoulder. "I know what you mean. Seems everyone's paired up, which leaves Harold Danforth's kids to wallow in their bad luck when it comes to relationships."

"Not all of us, Toby." She nodded toward the dance floor at their brother Jake and his wife, Larissa, holding each other close as the orchestra played a slow, mellow tune. "Jake looks pretty darned happy."

"He is happy. And I'm happy for him."

"Me, too."

Imogene didn't think Toby sounded all that enthusiastic, but then neither had she, and not because she didn't want Jake to be happy. It only served as a reminder of what she didn't have. She suspected the same held true for Toby.

Feeling the need for escape, Imogene stood and slipped the strap of her satin bag over her shoulder. "I think I'm going to grab some fresh air. Want to join me?"

Toby forked a hand through his dark hair. "I'll just sit here for a while. Maybe I can catch Mom and Dad between dances."

"Good luck."

Feeling suddenly stifled, Imogene shouldered her way through the masses until she reached the main hall. She made her way up the spiral staircase leading to the bedrooms. Many times she had played on these very stairs as a child, until the housekeeper had cautioned her and Victoria they would fall and break their necks if they didn't quit hanging off the wrought-iron banister. Of course, she and Tori had feigned innocence until Joyce had disappeared from sight. Then they would go back to whatever whimsical fantasy they'd concocted that day, be it swashbuckling pirates or freedom-fighting fairies.

The bittersweet memories lay heavily on Imogene's heart, only adding to her melancholy as she entered one of the myriad bathrooms to redo her lipstick and regain her calm. As she stared into the mirror, once more visions of Raf filtered into her mind. Raf making love to her in front of the mirrored wall. Raf holding her two nights ago until dawn. Raf watching her as she left him standing on the porch.

Her eyes welled with tears that she had tried so hard to keep. She let them fall at will down her cheeks for only a few moments before she chastised herself for her weakness. Raf would soon be a distant part of her life, a good—no, a great—memory she would keep with her always.

After repairing her makeup, Imogene stiffened her shoulders and her resolve to elevate herself beyond self-pity. She would go back downstairs and pretend to have a good time, maybe even dance with her dad if she could steal him away from her mom.

On the way down the hall, Imogene slowed her steps when she heard laughter and voices. Her uncle's voice, to be exact and that of a woman. Curiosity drove her to sneak a peak around the corner of the corridor that led to her uncle's suite. She only managed a quick glance before drawing back from shock. She'd gotten enough of a gander to recognize that Abraham Danforth, aspiring senatorial candidate, was not conducting business with his campaign manager, Nicola Granville. In fact, their conversation had ceased due to their mouths' preoccupation with a kiss. A very passionate kiss.

Imogene kept her back flattened against the wall as she

heard her uncle say, "I need to be with you, Nicola. Only for a while."

Even after the bedroom door opened then closed, she still didn't move as her mind tried to register what she'd just witnessed. Obviously Uncle Abe hadn't been concentrating solely on his campaign. And if anyone found out that he was cavorting with a member of his staff, then that would mean more scandal for an already scandal-ridden campaign.

Imogene decided then and there to keep his secret. It certainly wasn't her place to reveal what she now knew. At least he had good taste, she thought as she headed back to the stairs. Nicola Granville was a knock-out redhead, but she had to be at least fifteen years Abraham's junior. However, Uncle Abraham at fifty-five had more charisma and good looks than many men half his age. And obviously he wasn't ready to be put out to pasture.

Pasture—the stables, Raf. Every thought still centered on her dark prince who obviously couldn't be banished anymore than the spirits that still stalked the halls of Crofthaven. Now Imogene had another personal ghost to deal with aside from Tori, just as Raf still dealt with his wife's ghost.

Imogene consulted her watch as she descended the staircase. Now nearing 10:00 p.m., she decided to go home as soon as the honored guests departed for their honeymoon. But as she reached the last spiral turn, she glanced up and halted well short of her goal.

A man stood at the bottom of the banister dressed in a standard black tuxedo, his hands hidden in his pockets, his hair, dark as moonless midnight, now concealed by a white cloth secured by an ornate band. Imogene knew that about him just like she knew the faint round birthmark on his right hip, how he liked to be touched, how he sounded when he said her name. He looked every bit the desert prince, darkly handsome, mysterious, a heartbreaker of the first order. Imogene knew that well, too, because her own heart was breaking, seeing him there looking so beautiful. And she had no idea why he had come.

His magnetic gray eyes drew her forward and she felt as if she floated down the remaining stairs. When she stood before him, he held out his hand to her, which she took without the slightest hesitation. No words passed between them as she turned and led him through the ballroom and out onto the verandah that overlooked the front lawn.

Once there, she faced Raf, yet before she could ask him why he was there, he said, ''It was always you.''

''I don't understand,'' she said, and she didn't. The only thing she could comprehend was his unexpected presence and how strongly he affected her.

He reached out and tucked her hair behind her ear, then toyed with the diamond-drop earring in her lobe. ''The last night we were together, you were adamant that I make love to *you,* as if you believed someone else had come between us. That was not true. It has always been you. Only you.''

Imogene found it difficult to breathe, much less speak. ''But I thought—''

''That when I made love to you, I was making love with my wife. Nothing could be further from the truth.'' He gestured to the ornate bench in the corner of the verandah. ''Sit with me for a while. I need to explain the circumstances of my previous marriage.''

When she heard the pain in his voice, saw it in his expression, Imogene wasn't certain she wanted to hear it now. ''Does it really matter, Raf? Maybe you were right, the past belongs in the past.''

''My past will not be settled until you know everything.''

As they sat on the bench side by side, Imogene listened quietly while Raf explained the marriage arrangement, his wife's resentment and her subsequent death when he refused to discuss divorce.

"She never wanted me to touch her," he continued. "Everything we did together was out of obligation, not out of love. She died hating me."

Only now did everything come together for Imogene. Only now did it all make sense. "So that's why you were so determined we take it slowly?"

"Yes. Both with the riding and our lovemaking. I needed to make sure you were safe on the horse and willing in my bed."

"I think I proved to you several times I was willing."

Finally he smiled. A small one, but well worth his effort, in Imogene's opinion. "I had to be certain. I vowed I would not make love to a woman who did not want my attentions."

"I did, Raf." She still did. She also needed the answer to another question. "Is that the only reason you came here, to offer an explanation?"

He brought her hands to his lips for a kiss before resting them in his lap. "I came here tonight to amend my offer."

Imogene's heart tumbled to her toes. She had so hoped he'd come because he'd missed her. "Amend it in what way?"

"I wish to offer you more. A partnership."

"In the stable?"

"Yes. I would be willing to give you half the interest."

"Why on earth would you want to do that?"

"I spoke with the Granthams yesterday. They informed me that you have left your employer. They also told me you convinced them to sign on with BáHar's syndication. You have proven you have the stable's best interests at heart."

And he was still deeply engrained in her heart. "My way of repaying you for your instruction. It was the least I could do."

"There is something else you could do for me." He

lowered his eyes to their joined hands. "I am afraid the last time I did this it only involved signing papers."

"You've had a partner before?"

He lifted his dark gaze to hers. "I am not referring to only the business. I would like you to be more than only a business partner. I would like you to be my wife. If I am not assuming too much in believing you would do me the honor."

Imogene wanted to scream, "Yes!" But not until she had one more question answered. "If you mean you're assuming that I'm in love with you, my answer would be a definite yes. But how do you feel about me?"

He wore his heart in his eyes when he said, "You are the most strong-willed woman I know. The most passionate and beautiful woman I have encountered. And the only woman I have ever loved."

Imogene could do nothing but stare at him since speaking was impossible due to the boulder in her throat.

He thumbed away a tear that slipped from the corner of her eye. "Imogene Danforth, will you marry me?"

"Yes." She gave him a smile and the last of her heart. "On one condition."

"Whatever you ask of me, I will honor that as long as you agree."

She laughed through her tears. "Never, ever call me Imogene again."

"You will have my promise, Genie."

As he took her into his arms, it began to rain. A steady deluge that seemed to wash away the past and resurrect the time they had spent together in discovery of each other and their love. The rain intensified, and so did Raf's kiss—a kiss that held all the passion Imogene had come to know so well in his arms, and a newfound emotion she was only beginning to realize.

After a time Raf broke the kiss and said, "Perhaps we

should return to the party so that you can say a proper goodbye.''

Imogene kissed his cheek. ''I hate goodbyes. As far as I'm concerned, I don't intend to have any more in the near future.''

''Then we should return inside before we ruin your dress. And then we should return to the stables so that I might remove it, slowly.''

''That definitely sounds like a plan.''

They came inside out of the rain, arms around waists until they entered to find a crush of people gathered in the main hall. Before Imogene could register what was happening, a hand grabbed her arm and tugged her forward. ''Go up to the front of the crowd and take your place. Tina's about to toss the bouquet.''

Imogene glanced at her mother, who seemed to be oblivious to the fact that her daughter was soaked to the skin. But Imogene wasn't oblivious to the fact that she'd been set up when the bouquet landed in her arms to resounding applause.

Imogene tossed the flowers back over one shoulder to a flurry of activity behind her. No doubt, a few belles had seen their chance and grabbed it and the flowers. Frankly, Imogene didn't care about anything but getting out of there with Raf.

''Why did you do that?'' her mother asked. ''And why do you look like a drowned rat?''

Imogene laughed. ''I just came out of the rain and that's why I don't need the blasted bouquet.''

Miranda frowned. ''You are making no sense whatsoever.''

Imogene glanced behind her to see Raf standing back from the crowd, his tuxedo dotted with rain and his head now uncovered. ''It will all make sense if you follow me.''

She hooked her arm through her mother's and worked

her way back through the crowd while everyone stared at her as if she'd stripped naked. Once she reached Raf, she stopped and sent him a smile. "Raf Shakir, this is my mother, Miranda Danforth. Mother, is this my fiancé, Raf Shakir."

Her mother stared at Raf then leveled a wide-eyed gaze on Imogene. "I beg your pardon?"

Imogene left her mother's side to take Raf's hand. "I'll give you details later. Right now, we have better things to do."

As they turned and walked away, Miranda called out, "Imogene Danforth, you can't leave now after telling me something like that. Where are you going?"

Imogene regarded her mother over one shoulder and winked. "We're going to go find a wine cellar."

Epilogue

As the afternoon reception on the front lawn droned on under overcast skies, Raf stood apart from the wedding guests and watched his new wife work the crowd like the consummate businesswoman she would always be. But now she was his partner, his life, his all.

They had made their commitment official only a few hours ago in a simple ceremony inside the house, before an ''intimate'' gathering of 150 friends, associates and Genie's abundant family. Raf had requested they go away to be married, but he had not been able to refuse Genie when she had asked if he minded a real wedding. At least this time he had wed a woman who had been there of her own accord, not through obligation. A woman who had willingly demonstrated the true meaning of love when she had agreed to be with him for all time.

Having had his fill of his wife's absence, Raf made his way to Genie's side to intervene in her conversation with a portly, gray-haired gentleman and his doting younger wife.

"Thank you, Mr. Worth," Genie said as Raf slipped his arm around her waist and tugged her close to his side. "We'll send you the information as soon as we return from our honeymoon."

"Most definitely," Raf said. "Now, if you will excuse us."

Without giving Genie time to issue a protest, Raf pulled her across the lawn and toward the stables.

"Where are we going?" she said, holding up her dress as they entered the aisle. "I'm going to get my dress dirty."

"Not if I remove it," he said without slowing his steps.

At the bottom of the staircase leading to the apartment, he gathered her into his arms and took the stairs two at a time, driven by his impatience, his desire. He released her only long enough to open the door before carrying her across the threshold, a tradition Doris had informed him was absolutely necessary, otherwise the marriage was not valid. Of course, Raf had not believed her, but he was not willing to test his luck.

Once inside, he slid Genie to her feet and held her close to his racing heart. She smiled up at him and asked, "Why did you bring me here?"

"First, because I could no longer tolerate not having you alone. Second, because we have not made love in here. And lastly, if I had left you to your devices, you would have sold all the shares in BáHar before evening's end."

Her glaze faltered. "Actually, I already have."

"This does not surprise me."

She sought his eyes again. "Are you angry with me?"

He touched the corner of her mouth, one of his favorite spots to kiss. The other was covered by the dress, something he planned to remedy soon. "Never. Now we will have plenty of time to concentrate on other things for the next two weeks while in Italy.''

She loosened his tie as if entertaining the same ideas. ''I can't wait.''

''We will leave first thing tomorrow morning.''

''I mean I *can't* wait.'' With a vibrant grin on her beautiful face, she worked the buttons on his coat and slipped it off his shoulders. ''I don't see any reason why we can't take a break for a few minutes to start the honeymoon.''

''I could not agree more. But first I have a question.''

She began undoing the buttons on his shirt. ''Okay. Ask away.''

''Are you interested in breeding?''

She released the last button and ran her hands over his chest. ''With the right stud, I might be. As long as it doesn't involved any kind of dummies or teasing mares. Just you and me, babe, doing what comes naturally.''

''Then you do want children?''

She raised her gaze to his and he saw his future there. ''Yes, Raf, I do. At least six.''

He frowned. ''Six?''

''Yeah. Six. Ali said it's a nice, even number. He also said with that many, you're assured that at least one will take care of you in your old age.''

Raf could not suppress his laughter. ''Ali is a wise man. However, I hope I will have the energy to father six children.''

She worked his fly with deft fingers. ''I have no doubt you will.''

''I said 'father' six children, Genie. Not conceive them. I assure you I will be up to that task for many years.''

Genie freed him and ran a slow fingertip along his length, invoking his total arousal. ''I believe you are up for it now.''

Fueled by his passion for her, by his vast love for her,

Raf divested her of the simple satin wedding gown and removed the rest of his clothes. But before he could carry her to the nearby bedroom, a rap sounded at the door.

Raf groaned with frustration. "What is it!"

"It is Ali, Sheikh. The bride's mother wishes to know when you will cut the cake. The crowd is growing restless."

So was Imogene since Raf had already starting touching her everywhere she liked to be touched. "Tell her to give us an hour and keep the champagne flowing. That should keep them—" she gasped when Raf found the right spot with one gifted finger "—happy."

"As you wish, Your Highness."

"Your Highness?" Imogene said when Raf swept her off her feet and into his arms.

"Yes, Genie. You are a princess now."

As Raf carried her down the hall, she laid her head against his strong chest. "And you are definitely my prince, especially when you're being so charming to my mother. She is totally smitten with you. And my dad really likes you, too. Now, my brothers, they're going to be a little harder to win over since I'm their little sister." And if only the other little sister had been there today, watching Imogene marry the man she loved. If only…

Raf laid her down on the patchwork quilt covering the bed and held her face in his palms. "We will continue to search for her, Genie."

Once more Raf had read her well, just one more thing she loved about him. "It's okay, Raf. I'm still going to hold on to that hope. It will be much easier now that I have you to hold on to."

His features seemed so solemn for such a wonderful time. "As much as I would like to finish this, I would not blame you if you wish to return to your family. You have my blessing, if that is what you want."

She lifted his hand and surveyed the plain gold band that matched hers, symbols that they belonged together. "You're my family, too, Raf. I want to be with you right now. Only you. Because I love you more than you know."

"I love you as well, Genie. Always and completely."

The proof shone through when Raf made love to Imogene, not once closing his eyes, dispelling all her doubts that she was the only one on his mind, in his heart, in his life.

In the aftermath he said her name on a whisper, touched her with reverence, gave her the greatest pleasure she had known when he told her he loved her again.

And as they held each other, contented, satisfied, it began to rain.

"Thanks to tropical storm season, it looks like we won't be leaving here anytime soon," Imogene said. "I wouldn't want to ruin my dress."

Raf smiled the smile that had been partially responsible for Imogene's final fall into love. "Rest assured, Genie, I will never leave you. I would not want to ruin my life."

Imogene didn't worry about the abandoned and probably drenched wedding guests, or her future, or the things she couldn't control. She only wanted to stay in her husband's arms, making more memories to bring out on a rainy day.

And she hoped for many more rainy days to come.

*   *   *   *   *

Watch for COWBOY CRESCENDO
by Cathleen Galitz,
the next book in DYNASTIES: THE DANFORTHS,
available from
Silhouette Desire this July.

Silhouette Desire

DYNASTIES : THE DANFORTHS

**A family of prominence...
tested by scandal, sustained by passion.**

COWBOY
CRESCENDO
(Silhouette Desire #1591)

by Cathleen Galitz

Newly hired nanny Heather Burroughs quickly
won over Toby Danforth's young son with her
warmth and humor, but Toby's affection was
harder to tap into. This sizzling cowboy was
still reeling from his disastrous divorce and
certainly wasn't looking for a new bride.
Could Heather lasso this lone rancher
and get him to settle down?

*Available July 2004
at your favorite retail outlet.*

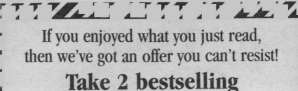

If you enjoyed what you just read,
then we've got an offer you can't resist!

Take 2 bestselling love stories FREE!

Plus get a FREE surprise gift!

Clip this page and mail it to Silhouette Reader Service™

IN U.S.A.
3010 Walden Ave.
P.O. Box 1867
Buffalo, N.Y. 14240-1867

IN CANADA
P.O. Box 609
Fort Erie, Ontario
L2A 5X3

YES! Please send me 2 free Silhouette Desire® novels and my free surprise gift. After receiving them, if I don't wish to receive anymore, I can return the shipping statement marked cancel. If I don't cancel, I will receive 6 brand-new novels every month, before they're available in stores! In the U.S.A., bill me at the bargain price of $3.57 plus 25¢ shipping and handling per book and applicable sales tax, if any*. In Canada, bill me at the bargain price of $4.24 plus 25¢ shipping and handling per book and applicable taxes**. That's the complete price and a savings of at least 10% off the cover prices—what a great deal! I understand that accepting the 2 free books and gift places me under no obligation ever to buy any books. I can always return a shipment and cancel at any time. Even if I never buy another book from Silhouette, the 2 free books and gift are mine to keep forever.

225 SDN DNUP
326 SDN DNUQ

Name	(PLEASE PRINT)	
Address	Apt.#	
City	State/Prov.	Zip/Postal Code

* Terms and prices subject to change without notice. Sales tax applicable in N.Y.
** Canadian residents will be charged applicable provincial taxes and GST.
  All orders subject to approval. Offer limited to one per household and not valid to current Silhouette Desire® subscribers.
  ® are registered trademarks of Harlequin Books S.A., used under license.

DES02   ©1998 Harlequin Enterprises Limited

Silhouette® Desire®

COMING NEXT MONTH

#1591 COWBOY CRESCENDO—Cathleen Galitz
Dynasties: The Danforths
Newly hired nanny Heather Burroughs quickly won over Toby Danforth's young son with her warmth and humor, but Toby's affection was harder to tap into. This sexy cowboy was still reeling from his disastrous divorce and wasn't looking to involve himself in any type of relationship. Could Heather lasso this lone rancher into settling down?

#1592 BEST-KEPT LIES—Lisa Jackson
The McCaffertys
Green-eyed P.I. Kurt Striker was hired to protect Randi McCafferty and her baby against a mysterious attacker. After being run off the road by this veiled villain, Randi had the strength to survive any curve life threw her. But did she have the power to steer clear of her irresistibly rugged protector?

#1593 MISS PRUITT'S PRIVATE LIFE—Barbara McCauley
Secrets!
Brother to the groom Evan Carter was immediately attracted to friend of the bride and well-known television personality Marcy Pruitt. While helping to pull the wedding together, they found themselves falling into a scandalous affair. But when Miss Pruitt's private life became public knowledge, would their shared passion result in a wedding of their own?

#1594 STANDING OUTSIDE THE FIRE—Sara Orwig
Stallion Pass: Texas Knights
Former Special Forces colonel and sexy charmer Boone Devlin clashed with Erin Frye over the ranch she managed and he had recently inherited. The head-to-head confrontation soon turned into head-over-heels passion. This playboy made it clear that nothing could tame him—but could an unexpected pregnancy change that?

#1595 BABY AT *HIS* CONVENIENCE—Kathie DeNosky
She wanted a strong, sexy man to father her child—and waitress Katie Andrews had decided that Jeremiah Gunn fit the bill exactly. Trouble was, Jeremiah had some terms of his own before he'd agree to give Katie what she wanted…and that meant becoming his mistress….

#1596 BEYOND CONTROL—Bronwyn Jameson
Free-spirited Kree O'Sullivan had never met a sexier man than financier Sebastian Sinclair. Even his all-business, take-charge attitude intrigued her. Just once she wanted Seb to go wild—for her. But when the sizzling attraction between them began to loosen *her* restraints, she knew passion would soon spiral out of control…for both of them.

SDCNM0604